A Courtship in the Highlands

Thistle and Rose
Book 2

Kate Robbins

ARE YOU SIGNED UP FOR DRAGONBLADE'S BLOG?

You'll get the latest news and information on exclusive giveaways, exclusive excerpts, coming releases, sales, free books, cover reveals and more.

Check out our complete list of authors, too!

No spam, no junk. That's a promise!

Sign Up Here

www.dragonbladepublishing.com

Dearest Reader;

Thank you for your support of a small press. At Dragonblade Publishing, we strive to bring you the highest quality Historical Romance from some of the best authors in the business. Without your support, there is no 'us', so we sincerely hope you adore these stories and find some new favorite authors along the way.

Happy Reading!

CEO, Dragonblade Publishing

Additional Dragonblade books by Author Kate Robbins

Thistle and Rose Series
A Courtship at Linlithgow (Book 1)
A Courtship in the Highlands (Book 2)

Dedication

For Sam and Spinelli

CHAPTER ONE

OFFERING HER BEST curtsey, Agnes Sinclar dared peeking upward to observe the countenance of the man her father had raved about for a fortnight. She'd not seen her uncle John in many years before this visit, but according to her father, his knowledge of the king's court and its goings on was unmatched among their acquaintances. Agnes found that odd, considering her father was Earl of Caithness and her uncle held no such title.

In any case, Agnes was fascinated to learn of King James's court, especially considering her father had secured a place for her among the queen's ladies in waiting while she summered at Stirling Castle. To sit with royalty morn and eve was something of which she'd only ever dreamed. Aye, she was an earl's daughter, but theirs was a more casual existence by most noble standards. They held few major gatherings throughout the year, mostly only focusing on the interests of the townsfolk. Beltane, Samhain, and Winter Solstice feasts and festivals were planned for months and showed little variety from year to year. The things she'd heard about King James's court were almost unimaginable.

Agnes couldn't wait to see more of the world. Her father had insisted on her arriving at Stirling Castle in a carriage, though he conceded she could ride her horse for a portion of the journey. She would thank him for it was how he had put it. Her mother had insisted she ride in the carriage the whole way, but in the end and after a bit of a row, they agreed she would ride for a portion of the day and then take respite in the carriage.

"You have grown much since I last saw you, niece."

"That is quite interesting, uncle, for I recall you being much taller," she said with a grin.

His brows drew together for a moment before saying, "Aye, and it appears you have your mother's cheek about you too. That will not serve you well in the queen's court, Lady Agnes."

At eighteen summers, Agnes did not feel she needed scolding from him or anyone else. Still, he apparently knew all there was to know about the court so she would bite her tongue for now.

Wasn't the whole point of her going to court to find a husband? Would they all expect her to be submissive? Considering her parents' marriage could be considered quite spirited, this was a new concept.

"Now, now, John, you need not frighten her. It is quite an honor to be part of the queen's entourage and since Agnes and the queen are only a year apart in age, I am certain they will get along well."

"I am not frightened, father. I respect Uncle John's knowledge of court and look forward to learning more on our journey to Stirling."

"Very well, daughter, off you go with your mother to finish packing. John and I have many things to discuss."

Agnes glanced once more at her uncle before leaving the great hall. His entire demeanor was not what she expected. He had the look of a man who trusted no one with his secrets, and she was certain he had a few under lock and key.

"How well do you know my uncle?" she asked her mother when they were out of earshot.

"As well as any woman can know her husband's siblings when they live so far away. I've never known him as a soft and warm sort of man if that's what you're asking. But you will be perfectly safe with him. Now, never you mind your uncle. We must ensure you have enough gowns packed, and I will see to it you have several more made once you arrive at Stirling. The seamstresses there are not as good as in Edinburgh, but they will do quite nicely. There will be many balls and festivals soon, so I expect there will be a waiting list."

"Oh wait, I forgot to tell you, father mentioned yesterday that Uncle had already secured a seamstress for me who can start on my gowns as soon as I arrive."

Her mother stopped fussing with Agnes's chests and stood tall. Her chin lifted a little as she said, "Well it appears he's thought of everything now, hasn't he?"

"It appears he has," she said. "And you are certain this is a good path for me, I mean aside from me finally seeing something other than the Sinclair Bay and the sea sprites who frolic when the moon is full."

Her mother smiled softly. "Aye, my sweet wee lassie. I would not be letting ye go otherwise."

Agnes had not been a wee lassie for a long time but still loved it when her mother addressed her so.

"And does my uncle have your and father's blessing should I find a suitable match?"

"He does not have full blessing, nay. And if he tells you so he is not being truthful. Your father and I have asked him to be your guardian and attendant at all social functions. He may offer guidance and advice on some of the people you will meet, but it is not up to him to have a final say on whom you will marry."

Her mother placed her hands on her hips, and it was clear to Agnes she'd struck a chord.

"Maybe this business is folly from the start. Your father and I should be presenting you at court, not your uncle. I should go speak with your father."

"Nay, Mother, that is not necessary. I am certain all will be well. I just want to be sure of your intentions for me. You have been more than patient with me over the past two years with rejection after rejection from me. I promise you, I will make you proud and honor the Sinclair name."

"I don't doubt your integrity for a moment," she said and sighed. "I don't know if it's ever easy for a parent to watch their child leave their home, even if for just a few weeks. With your older brothers gone and in their own homes, I now only have little Hugh left to dote on."

Agnes couldn't help but smile at the thought. At twelve summers, Hugh had always been everyone's bairn and he made no attempt to prove everyone wrong at every turn. As a wee lad, Agnes used to lift him up to the window enclosure so he could peek out through the narrow opening to watch the sea crashing against the rocks dozens of feet below. She'd tell him stories about Bregdi, the great sea creature that would sneak up on poor sailors in the night, whisking them away to never be heard from again.

She'd miss those times, but this was her time to discover who she was to be in the world and where this adventure would take her. She could not predict what was to come, but she couldn't wait to find out.

Her mother left her to finish selecting the items she wanted to take with her. Many of her favorite gowns lay strewn across her bed. Yards of finely stitched velvet and brocade in other colors, but most in her favorite pale blue, like her eyes, her mother always said.

She turned away from the gowns and gazed out at the sea from her window. What did this journey have in store for her? Would she find a suitable husband? What would he be like? Did she even know what she wanted?

One thing was for certain: She would not be happy with a man with whom she could not openly speak. Her parents had enough respect for one another that they spoke their opinions fully and frequently, even if they differed. Nay, she wanted a partner with whom she could converse and disagree and who would respect her interest in culture and art and music. She wanted to experience the world and its glorious offerings.

THE IMAGE OF Stirling Castle rising high above the plains below was a sight that would never tire William Graham. He'd visited this castle often with his father since his own home, Mugdock Castle was only twenty odd miles away. The setting sun at his back cast a long shadow of his horse and himself as they trotted through Stirling toward the castle. In the coming days this place would buzz with excitement as the king commenced his summer season of festivities. Long known to possess a penchant for the extravagant, the king tried to outdo himself every year and in the four years since William had been permitted to attend the balls, he could attest to the king's efforts outshining anything else he'd experienced.

Since his father's passing a few years back, he'd accepted all invitations from the king. But he had not for the most part allowed himself to be swept up, as others had, with the pressure of his title and family responsibilities. This season would be different. He'd finally secured a marriage for his sister to one Connor Munroe over the winter, not that there was anything wrong with his sister besides being rather selective. He would never blame her or force her into any arrangement to which she opposed, but he was relieved nonetheless and with only two much younger siblings to have wed at some point, these next few weeks would be a reprieve for him. His sister's husband was an unremarkable man, though he did come with lands of his own gifted to him from his father. She appeared pleased and that was all he could have hoped for.

William had hoped to convince his mother to join him and bring some joy back into her life as well. He'd nearly convinced her, but in the end, she chose to find comfort in her favorite spot in the garden to have her daily conversations with her husband's stone marker.

Dismounting, he passed the reins to a stable hand and was

met by the king's chamberlain who greeted him with a cheeky grin that was commonplace for this man.

"Fin! I am unsure what has afforded me the lofty honor of your escort, but I am pleased it is so."

"Aye, my lord. His Majesty offered me the choice of those I would assist upon arrival, and I was selective in doing so."

"Then the honor is doubly mine. Even my father was only waited on by a gentleman usher," he said and placed his thumb and finger on his chin, narrowing his eyes. "Unless you both are up to something."

Fin raised his brows and shrugged his shoulders. "I am not privy to the king's plans," he said with a smile. "Now, if you will allow me, I will show you to your chamber. Would you like a bath drawn? The king will take his meal with the queen in their apartment this eve, but I am instructed to bring you whatever you would like for your own satisfaction."

"Nice change of subject, Fin. But, aye, I am saddle weary and could do with a hot meal."

"Right this way, my lord," Fin said and led them from the courtyard through to the guest chambers.

There was plenty of hustle and bustle all around as chamber maids moved about with linens and ushers moved their respective guests to the assigned chambers. William's chamber overlooked the inner courtyard and housed a large four-post bed with a dark-crimson brocade cap. The dark wooden posts were ornately carved with thistles, roses, unicorns, and lions. He'd passed on the bath but now regretted it as the hours of riding had taken their toll. Fin had just gone to order a platter of supper when a knock sounded at the door. Upon direction, the door opened revealing several men carrying steaming buckets of water. Apparently, the king would see to his guest's comfort whether they wished it or not. The men poured the water into the tub William hadn't even realized was off in a smallish side chamber. He would have to remember that little trick for his own chamber at Mugdock Castle. It would save time and effort if the tub simply remained and only the water had to be transported. Did all the guest chambers at Stirling possess their own bath?

Before he had another moment to contemplate the king's luxuries, Fin returned followed by two more servants who carried a platter filled with something aromatic and steaming and a tankard with goblets. Was all that meant for him?

"My lord, would you prefer to take your bath before or after your meal?" Fin asked.

He'd prefer to do both together, but was reluctant to be so bold in his host's home, and so replied, "I will eat and then bathe. I am certain once I relax I will only want to retire."

"Very well, I shall return after a while to assist you."

Once the door closed, William turned his attention to the food. The aroma coming from the platter was undeniably intoxicating. He removed his belt and pulled his tunic over his head then removed his leine. Sitting by the hearth, he sampled the meat and sopped up some of the juices with the bread. Roasted boar, his favorite. He'd have to seek out the cook to ask how he'd gotten the skin so perfectly crisp with the meat so tender and juicy. He poured a goblet of the liquid into the tankard and was pleased it was a medium ale and not something light and with little flavor which seemed to be the growing preference these days.

After about an hour, Fin returned with two more steaming buckets of water. William had been so engrossed in his meal, he'd not thought about the water cooling.

Moving over to the tub, he kicked off his boots and untied the string holding his trews about his waist and then slipped them off.

The first sensation of the warm water was heavenly. He'd not ridden that distance in quite a long time and though he considered himself strong and healthy, riding all day would wear anyone out.

He sat back in the tub enjoying how the perfect heat soothed his aching muscles.

"Do you require any assistance washing, my lord?" Fin asked.

"Nay, you may attend your other guests. I will be in bed before much longer."

"Do you wish the water removed this eve or in the morn, my lord?"

"In the morning is fine, Fin. Thank you for having the water prepared anyway," he said. "You are quite proficient at your job."

"Aye, I am," he said with a chuckle. "Tomorrow will commence the festivities so sleep well, my lord. 'Twill be an early rise."

"Thank you, Fin," he said. "I look forward to it."

"Oh, and my lord?"

William turned his head to look at Fin.

"You need not worry the king has anything planned for you to embarrass you. He merely wants to reward excellence in service to the crown."

Fin's demeanor, which was usually light and jovial, had taken a turn toward somber. His gaze was cast downward and his normal smile disappeared.

"The king has always had our full support. He need not fear that changing. Has something happened?"

"Not yet," he said.

William sat up straighter. "Has there been some kind of threat?"

"I promised the king I would let him tell you himself," Fin said, now wringing his hands.

"Then you shall obey your king and understand I will say nothing to him unless he says so to me."

"Thank you, my lord. I know I can depend on you, and the king knows that as well."

With that he left the chamber, leaving William with more questions than answers. It was no secret the king had enemies near and far. All the previous kings had, and he supposed that would be true anywhere. But in all the years he'd known Fin, he'd never seen the man without a smile or a kind word. Normally so full of life, he was now almost afraid. This threat must have serious grounds.

He would find out soon enough once he met with the king on the morrow. For now, he sat back in the tub and enjoyed the heat. He tilted his head back and closed his eyes, thinking of all the known enemies of the king and all the ways they could harm him in the middle of a festival.

William woke with a start a time later as the water had cooled significantly. He stepped out of the tub and dried himself off enough and then slipped in between the cool sheets. The heavy quilts on the bed pulled him back to slumber within seconds. His last thought was of the king.

CHAPTER TWO

A GNES COULDN'T HELP but grin as she poked her head out of the carriage window to feast her eyes on Stirling Castle in the distance. To say her journey with her uncle had been strange was an understatement. Instead of telling her all about the gentry, he spent more time giving her a history lesson about the previous king and how the current one had betrayed him over some such thing.

Most of the time she tuned him out when he'd go on and on about loyalty. Och, she was more interested in the ladies' fashions and who was expected to court whom. Now with the castle in sight, a small knot formed in her stomach as she did not feel prepared at all for what was before her. She was well aware of the basics, but not knowing how many other ladies would attend the queen or from whence they hailed was disconcerting.

"Remember what I told you," her uncle said riding up alongside the carriage.

He'd told her many things, most of which she considered useless. "Aye, Uncle, I remember." No, she didn't.

"Agnes, 'tis imperative you remember everything I said. Do you vow it?"

She couldn't tell if he really expected her to recall all the things he'd said over the last several days while she was trying to enjoy her journey and grow some excitement for the adventure before her.

"Say it with me one time."

Say what?

"Loyalty is everything," he said.

She recalled then. Something he'd said last eve at the inn where they stayed near Inverness. *Your actions will always reveal where your loyalties lie. Loyalty is everything.* It was some kind of motto for these men he kept mentioning. The knot in her stomach grew and not because of any concern she had for meeting new people or what fashion they might prefer.

"Say it." His words drew her back to the present. His eyes narrowed and his mouth drew into a thin line. He glared at her hard in a way no one in her life ever had. Hair prickled at her nape.

She blinked at him a couple times then whispered, "Loyalty is everything."

The words were dirty in her mouth, yet she did not have a reason for why they felt wrong. There was something about the way his mouth curled when she said them that made her want to turn the carriage around and return to Grinigoe Castle.

But she would not let her uncle take away her first memories of Stirling Castle and her introduction to the king and queen.

As the carriage drew to a halt, a footman quickly opened her door and offered his hand to assist.

The moment her foot touched ground, another man stepped up to offer her his arm. "Lady Agnes," he said. "My name is Fin and I am the chamberlain here at Stirling Castle." His smile was warm and kind. "I trust your journey was uneventful."

"I will escort Lady Agnes to her chamber," her uncle interjected and held out his arm in an expectant way.

"That is very kind, sir, but the king himself insisted I see to Lady Agnes's every comfort as she prepares to meet Her Majesty."

"'Tis all well, Uncle," Anges said with as much of a comforting tone as she could muster. "I am certain the king knows what is best for his guests."

"Your usher will be here momentarily and will see to your every comfort as well, sir," Fin said.

"My chamber is adjacent to my niece, I expect?"

"Lady Agnes's chamber is near the queen's apartment along with the other ladies in waiting. I have prepared you comfortable accommodations in the men's wing," he said and then raised his hand to urge someone their way.

"Archie, see to it that Laird Sinclair is situated in the chamber we have set aside for him."

Archie appeared wide eyed and shook his head ever so slightly it was easy to miss if one were not paying attention.

"'Tis the one near Montrose," Fin offered and then to her uncle, he said, "Archie will see to your every need and will advise you of activities and mealtimes. There is already a copper tub in your chamber, and you may request to have it filled at any time."

Fin then bowed to her uncle with a little bit of a flourish clearly indicating dismissal. Did Fin know her uncle and dislike him? There appeared a hint of something that made her more valuable than him. Or was that just the way of things based on her status versus his? Sure he was still considered gentry, but with no formal title, though plenty of his own land, he was seen as lesser somehow. She didn't quite comprehend the inner workings of it all, but she knew enough that some people were treated differently depending on their name.

John owned untitled lands, making him a laird and allowing him to engage freely with gentry and nobility alike. But she didn't miss the underlying implication in this greeting.

Once her uncle left with Archie, Fin turned to her. "Now, Lady Agnes, let me have a good look at you." He sized her up and down and nodded. "My lady, you're a fair one for a catch, to be sure. I think plenty heads will turn at your entrance at tomorrow's ball."

"Thank you, Fin. I admit, I am a wee bit out of my element here. We don't hold festivities quite this elaborate."

She looked around them. The inner courtyard was filled with

what could be described as a market, but 'twas like none she'd ever encountered. The entire perimeter was filled with carts topped with fabrics and jewelry and pies and so many pastries her stomach growled loudly, though no one would hear with all the activity. Musicians played lively tunes and ladies wearing hundreds of beads danced around them. All her senses were on alert to the colors and textures and aromas enveloping her.

"There will be plenty of time to explore the market, later," Fin said beside her. "For now, let me show you to your chamber so you can rest up and pick out your gown to meet the queen at the evening meal."

"Will my chest be brought up this quickly?"

"Not quite," he said and grinned.

When he didn't offer any further detail, she didn't ask. If there was a surprise waiting for her, she didn't want to ruin it. She was certain of two things at that moment: She was grateful for the respite from her uncle, and she liked Fin. He was kind and funny, and something deep within her told her to trust him. She couldn't say the same about Uncle John.

They passed through the guest portion of the castle set aside for accommodations and on toward a separate wing Fin described as the king and queen's apartment. Within was her chamber along with the other five ladies with whom she would be responsible to entertain the queen and keep her company at times when the king was occupied with other duties or interests.

"But truth be told, his interest of late is very much all about her," Fin said with the side of his hand almost covering his mouth.

"And that's a good thing, aye? That they are in love. They are supposed to be, are they not?"

"Lady Agnes, you will soon learn that love stories are not always possible among the elite at the king's court."

Well, that was disappointing to hear.

"Oh, but not for you, Lady Agnes. I am certain you will find a perfect match."

His words were kind as was his expression, making it seem sincere, but somehow it appeared there was so much more he could tell her. Should she ask about the gentry? Would that be inappropriate considering she should know all about them?

"Now here we are, my lady," Fin said and opened the door wide. With a broad sweep of his hand he said, "This will be your chamber for the next several weeks. What do you think?"

What she thought was that her own bedchamber was a fishing stage compared to this one. Bright colorful tapestries adorned the walls in hues of the sky and of a stormy sea. Here and there pops of bright yellow and orange caught her eye until finally she spied the largest bed she'd ever seen with four thick pale wooden posts and a shiny blue cap. She resisted the urge to throw herself upon it.

"I can see you approve. In here," he said leading her to a side chamber with a copper tub lined with sheets of linen and a long table and bench. On the table were various vials in all shapes and sizes with many different colors and apparent textures; some were thick and pink, others were watery and purple. She could imagine the baths she would take here.

"Her Majesty enjoys being pampered and expects the same for her ladies."

"Fin?"

"Aye, Lady Agnes?"

"What is she like?"

"The queen?"

"Aye, no one would tell me anything about her."

"She is one year younger than you, and rather clever with a charming sense of humor. I believe you both will get along quite well."

"I do hope so. And I think I would like to consider you a friend as well."

"While it is unusual for one of the queen's ladies to befriend a member of household staff, I confess," he said with a grin, "I like you already."

Fin was a tall, thin man with his hair tied neatly at his nape and his clothing impeccably precise. She could see him being an excellent older brother. Though she was not attracted to him, she could see anyone being drawn to his kindness and the little hint of mischievousness that hid just under the surface. At least in this half-mad situation in which she found herself, she had one friend.

WILLIAM LISTENED TO the king's words with near disbelief. He supposed anything was possible, but after all this time?

"You are certain?" William asked again.

"Do you doubt your king's intelligence?"

"Put that way, no, Your Majesty. But it's been so long since we've heard from any of them."

"Aye, it has, and now they have a plan to make sure their voices are heard loud and clear."

"I just don't understand why now," William said, shaking his head and leaning back in his chair. They had been talking for a while before the king revealed his concerns. It was likely now he was not sure who to trust.

"Were you given names?"

"Aye, one we are fairly certain is involved and with him one who plans to attend my wife."

"And who is that?"

"Lady Agnes Sinclair. I'd received a missive from her father some months ago and upon speaking with my wife finally convinced her to keep a set of ladies for company and she agreed. Once word spread, other noble houses offered their kin to add to the entourage. As of now with Lady Agnes's arrival, the queen will have that one attend her and the rest in the coming days."

"Can't you just send her back?" He didn't quite mean to blurt the words, but did it make sense to keep the lady close and allow her access to the queen?

"My Lord Montrose, nothing in our world is quite that simple, which is why I've asked to speak with you. I have placed her uncle in the chamber adjacent to yours. He is a cunning man with lands but no title, by my design because of his rumored affiliation with those who still support my father. I do not know to what extent she is involved, or even he for that matter. I would like you to get to know them both and see what you can glean. I have other avenues at play as well, so if you are not up to the task, I will be disappointed, but I will understand. I know her parents are loyal to the crown, and I do not wish to risk damaging that relationship as they represent my interests in the north. So you see, 'tis delicate."

Delicate indeed when one is expected to sniff out a potential traitor in the form of an unmarried lady or a lesser laird. The latter could rarely be trusted.

"Your Majesty, I will of course do as you have bid, as always. And I will be discreet. I am not familiar with that family so an introduction would be required."

"I can offer assurance of that at this evening's meal. I will ensure you are seated together. I thank you, Montrose, for your continued loyalty to me and my family."

"You will always have it, Your Majesty, until I draw my last breath."

With that, the king dismissed William to his chamber to await the evening meal. He paced behind the closed door and wondered if this John Sinclair was next door at that moment plotting and scheming. Not thinking he'd hear anything, he placed his ear to the stone wall. Castles were notorious for cracks through which sounds could carry, but alas there was nothing.

Without any other option, and since the evening meal was hours away, William took himself off to explore the market and to distract himself from the growing worry about the level of threat the king faced. Were there other spies about plotting with Sinclair and his traitorous niece? What would he say when he met them? Did he possess the qualities needed to hold his tongue if aught was revealed to him? He hoped so.

CHAPTER THREE

AGNES SMILED TO herself as she gazed around the chamber. Three large chests and a wardrobe drew her attention and, unable to resist, she opened them just as a knock sounded at the door and Fin entered with servants who carried water for her bath.

"I see you have found your surprise," he said. "They are gifts from the queen, and her seamstress is on hand for any alterations that may be required."

Agnes lifted one out of the chest which was a thick brocade with gold stitching on deep gray-blue fabric.

"I think that is the one you should wear this evening," he said. "Your eyes are the color of ice, Lady Agnes. Aye, this one will do well."

She held the gown up to her body and turned toward the mirror. Her dark hair had been pinned up for comfort during the journey, but she pulled the pins out and let her tresses cascade around her shoulders. Fin was right; it was like this gown had been designed perfectly for her.

"How did the queen know which colors to choose?" she asked as she gazed into the chest to see many other dark and dramatic colors that she could envision would also match her well.

"We intercepted the missive your uncle sent to the seamstress in town and what can I say is, her majesty's seamstress is exceedingly talented at her job. Now," he said as he held out his hands for the gown, "let me hang this, and you are to let Cora here assist you with a bath and a rest up as the evening meal will be just a few short hours away and you will be her majesty's particular guest this evening."

"Thank you, Fin," she said trying to hide the nervousness threatening to let loose.

"You will be fine, Lady Agnes," he said and bowed to her before leaving the chamber.

She turned to Cora who wore a shy smile. "This way m'lady."

Agnes wasn't used to such a distinction between servants and the family. They were much more informal at Grinigoe, but she understood the necessity in this setting.

Cora helped her out of her traveling gown, which was mostly wool for warmth, though it was much warmer here at Stirling than up north. Beneath her gown she wore a linen shift and stockings. It was good to have it all removed and when she sank into the bath, she let the past days drain from her body. The maid washed her hair and limbs and though Agnes had bathed herself regularly, she was grateful for the assistance, having not quite realized just how tired she was.

At some point she drifted, but a little nudge from Cora roused her. "M'lady, if you are finished, I can dry you and turn back your covers. You have plenty of time for a nap and a respite before the evening meal."

That was the best thing she'd heard all day. Once Cora wrapped her hair in cloths and helped her with her dressing gown and into bed, she pulled the covers up and said, "I will return in an hour to work on your hair."

Agnes was convinced she'd just closed her eyes when Cora returned. She held a tray with cheese and bread and a goblet and tankard.

"Come to the fire, m'lady, and I will make you ready. I have brought some food for you in case you are hungry."

It appeared she knew what Agnes needed more than she knew herself. For as soon as she spied the platter her belly rumbled.

Taking a seat near the hearth, she gave herself over completely to Cora's preening. She'd always taken care with her appearance, but the way this maid curled and pinned her hair after brushing was somewhat fascinating. After a while and once her hair had dried fully, Cora removed the pins to reveal beautiful curls that hung around Agnes's shoulders and back. She then swept her hair from the sides of her face and pinned those curls loosely at her crown. The look was simple but elegant. She then took tiny gold beads that were strung together and pinned them to her hair forming a wreath.

When her hair was finished, it was time to begin the arduous task of getting dressed. Agnes usually dressed herself and was grateful for Cora's presence today, for she was not quite sure she could don this gown on her own.

From the tall wardrobe, Cora selected a shimmery garment and held it out to her. Agnes nearly gasped as she accepted the shift and felt the silky fabric; she was sure it would be like heaven on her skin. Slipping it over her head she tried to hide her excitement as the fabric caressed her curves. She turned from Cora as her nipples hardened. She'd never worn anything like this and wondered if all the ladies at court wore these.

"Is aught amiss, m'lady?"

Turning back to Cora, she said, "Nay, all is well. I just caught a chill, is all."

Cora's cheeks were pink and Agnes wondered if she understood the effect the garment had on her.

Moving more quickly now Cora helped Agnes step into first the under skirt and then the heavy outer skirt, securely tying them at her waist. Then came the rigid bodice which tied tightly at her back and pushed her breasts upward, and finally the outer bodice which formed a deep V at her waist with long sleeves that flowed with the folds of her skirt.

Just as she fastened a fine sapphire necklace around her neck, a knock sounded at the door and Fin entered.

His mouth opened wide for a moment before he composed himself and straightened his back. Holding out his arm, he said, "Lady Agnes, it is my pleasure to escort you to the great hall."

The time had come and taking one last look in the mirror, Agnes drew in a deep breath and accepted Fin's arm then left the chamber.

The gown was the heaviest she had ever worn and she prayed the hall was not too far away, lest she'd need a rest in between.

They meandered past all the chambers and down the stairs, through the still bustling inner courtyard, and then to the great hall. Its ornately decorated outside was nothing compared to the inside. At the head was a large tapestry of a unicorn and lion surrounded by dozens of roses and thistles. Below that was a large dais with a long table she was sure could seat half of the king's court. Long tables were also set perpendicular to the head table, and some people had already gathered and were standing in random groups conversing among themselves.

Agnes scanned the hall as Fin guided them through the beautifully decorated crowd. That was the only way she could think of them with their tall headdresses or hoods and more jewelry than she'd ever seen a single person wear. She noticed the abundance of flowers and decoration, her eyes drinking it all in. Her attention was drawn to the head table. The king and queen were not yet in attendance, and she was surprised when Fin led her to that table where a man stood, waiting.

Her breath caught in her throat. His eyes were bright and fixed on her. She could not tell the color, not quite brown, not quite green, but they were intense. *He* was intense as he held her gaze.

When they were just before him, she tilted her head up to see him, and Fin said, "Lord Montrose, may I introduce Lady Agnes Sinclair. Lady Agnes, this is Lord William Graham, the Right

Honorable Earl of Montrose."

Agnes's breath was still caught in her throat. She wasn't sure she could speak for she'd never encountered a man who had such a presence about him.

"Lady Agnes," he said in a deep voice that reminded her of the way her silk shift had caressed her skin. "It is my pleasure to make your acquaintance."

"My lord, the pleasure is mine," she said in a voice just above a whisper.

For what seemed like long, awkward moments they stared at one another until Fin made a sound sort of like a cough.

She tore her gaze from the earl's piercing stare she was sure reached her very soul. When she turned to Fin, he guided her to the long table and away from the earl. She could not help but look over her shoulder and was surprised he still gazed at her with the same intensity.

In the next moment, the earl was at her other side and to Fin said, "I will introduce her to their majesties. You may see about your other duties."

With that Fin bowed, offered her a small smile, and left them.

Of all the awkward moments she'd ever endured, this was by far the worst. This man who was like something out of a legend or myth had stolen her wits by his mere presence. She didn't know if she should be embarrassed by her reaction to him or mortified, but one thing was certain, she was enchanted.

THE FEELING OF her small hand on his arm sent electric jolts up his arm. William had to get himself under control, else he could never be around her and, as the king had said, glean intelligence. She was like a magnet for him from the moment she entered the hall. He was aware of her every move, of each item that appeared to captivate her. She'd captivated him. Politeness would dictate that he should have moved to them when they entered the hall, but he'd been rooted to his spot and could barely breathe as she approached. Once their gazes locked, he was powerless to do anything but stare at her.

But this was foolish; he couldn't be attracted to her and try to extract information from her at the same time. He was acting like an unseasoned school lad. Not that he was as active as some of his acquaintances, but he'd partaken in sport when it was available with no expectations. This woman conjured feelings of such fervor, he didn't quite know what to make of it. He pushed those thoughts to the side. He had to for now.

"I trust your journey was uneventful?" he asked her.

"Aye, my lord, and yours?"

He liked the way her cheeks grew pink after she said the words and looked like she wanted to swallow them. Maybe, it was not only he who was affected. He took in her demeanor with closer regard. Her expression was bright and he could see the intelligence in her eyes and, aye, curiosity there too. Was it possible the lady was innocent of all knowledge of a plot? He would expect that person to be cool and unrattled and that was not the air she had about her at all.

"My journey was uneventful and not near as long as yours."

"Pardon my ignorance, my lord, but from whence do you hail?"

"My home is about twenty miles from here. I understand your father is the Earl of Caithness."

"Aye, my lord. I am here with my uncle. My parents remain in the north."

She was free enough with that information.

"And I understand you are to attend the queen and you have not yet met."

"I confess, I have not, my lord."

"Then we shall remedy that right now," he said and placed his hand over hers guiding her toward the king and queen who had just entered the hall near the head table.

William smiled at the monarchs as they approached and could sense the tension rolling from Lady Agnes in waves. He instinctively squeezed her hand then regretted the inappropriate gesture of familiarity though it was almost involuntary.

"Your Majesties, may I introduce Lady Agnes Sinclair, daughter of the Earl of Caithness. Lady Agnes, may I present you to Their Graces King James and Queen Margaret."

William bowed and Lady Agnes curtseyed at the same time.

The queen moved forward and reached out her hands to Lady Agnes as she stood. "My Lady Agnes, you are more beautiful than we were told. I am pleased to make your acquaintance and expect to hear all about your life in the north and introduce you to as many courtesans as would please you. I have had few true friends since my time here and do understand that all this hustle and bustle is not for everyone. But I do hope it is to your liking."

"Aye, Your Majesty," Agnes said in a voice that was a little shaky. "I have never seen such grandeur."

With that comment the king stood a little taller. "The lady has good taste, it would seem. Now while the ladies become acquainted, Montrose, I have something I would discuss with you before the meal is served."

Lady Agnes looked at him then and offered a small smile. Was that a thank you? He was not quite sure. It was impossible to know a person's mind upon meeting them, but his instinct was that she was a genuinely good person. He hoped his instincts would prove truth.

Once off to the side the king asked, "Well? What is your first impression?"

What it was he would not fully reveal to the king. That he wanted to smell her hair and kiss those full lips of hers and explore the delights she hid under her gown. Nay, he would not share that with the king.

"She appears reserved, but there is an active mind behind those eyes. It is far too early to tell if she is innocent or an adept player in this whatever it is scheme of her uncle's."

"And have you met him yet?"

"I have not, but I suspect will through the course of the evening once the meal begins and he comes to find his niece."

"A logical assessment. Right, then let us enjoy our meal and let the game unfold before us."

William was seated to the right of the king and Lady Agnes seated to the queen's left. That meant they could not converse during the course of the meal, but he would stay close to her once the crowd mingled later on.

Before long, the tables were topped with more food than William had ever seen anywhere, but for at this king's gatherings. A suckling pig was placed before the king who appeared to enjoy watching one of the cooks sharpen his knife to carve the meat for his inspection and indicating to whom it would be offered. It was no surprise all the best cuts went first to his wife and then to Lady Agnes. After that he offered William and then filled his own trencher.

Steaming pots of stew and platters of bread and cheese and fruits were brought out one by one. William focused on enjoying the hospitality, but being ever aware of Lady Agnes and of the king.

William scanned the crowd for the lady's uncle and eventually found him near the end on the far side opposite. He stared hard at the head table and William couldn't make out if he even touched his food. There was a marked difference between his demeanor and that of his niece, giving William even more pause as to whether or not she was part of this.

"Do you see how fixated he is?" the king asked.

"Aye, I do."

"Quite interested in what is happening up here, I think."

"Your assessment mirrors my own, Your Majesty. Have you spoken with Fin and Archie? What are their thoughts?"

"I spoke with Fin. He believes she is *a creature of perfection* as he put it," the king said and chuckled. "She has bewitched our Fin, I think."

She'd bewitched more than Fin by William's estimation. More than a few gentlemen glanced in her direction repeatedly only to glance away again.

William and the king enjoyed the remainder of the meal in silence quietly observing those around them. Once the meal ended, the king offered his welcome to his guests and invited them to explore the market in the inner courtyard.

"We have vendors from near and as far away as France. I do believe the ladies will be particularly interested in the delicate fabrics and fragrances," he told his guests.

Once the king and queen stood and their chairs were pulled back, the crowd did the same and began making their way out of the stuffy hall and toward the market.

William waited for the king and queen to link arms and move to the side entrance then offered his arm to Lady Agnes. Her eyes were bright and her expression soft as if a weight had been lifted from her.

"Did you enjoy your meal, Lady Agnes?"

"Aye, I did, my lord. 'Twas the grandest feast I have ever attended."

Her comment made William smile. She appeared full of wonder.

"Would you do me the honor of exploring the market with me?"

She stopped and looked around for a moment. "I really should find my uncle as I am sure he would wish to accompany me."

"That he would," the uncle said from behind her.

Lady Agnes jumped at his voice which was a peculiar reaction if they were in collaboration willingly.

"Uncle John, allow me to introduce Lord William Graham, the Earl of Montrose. My lord, this is my uncle John Sinclair."

The man did not smile and when he bowed as he should, it was so quick, if William had blinked he'd have missed it. He didn't need to be a scholar to understand there was a dislike held by this man that he was not trying hard to conceal. Interesting.

CHAPTER FOUR

S HE WOULD HAVE much preferred to stroll through the market with the earl, however, she was well aware her uncle would never allow that. And truly her parents wouldn't either.

"You appear to have befriended the queen rather quickly," he said in her ear. His words were spoken quickly and in a sharp tone.

"I thought that was why I was here, to become one of her ladies and serve her," Agnes said quietly and couldn't help feeling a little defensive.

"You will remember what I told you and why you are here or else."

Agnes didn't want to know what else, but she would take every advantage to spend more time with the queen than her uncle.

Once outside she tried to focus more on the items on display than her uncle whose coldness seeped into her heart. He was not here to help her find a suitable match. He had his own agenda, and, for the life of her, she was certain it had to do with those mundane stories he'd told her on their travels. She could kick herself now for not paying closer attention.

"One turn about the market and then you will take your leave and retire for the evening."

"That is not my decision to make, Uncle. The queen will

dismiss me when she is no longer in need of my company."

Agnes had just met the woman and had spent a lovely meal with her. She liked Queen Margaret very much and could see them becoming good friends. She was not about to toss that out the window because of her uncle's opinions.

"You will do as you are told and I don't care what kind of lie you make up, but you will make your excuses when I tell you." He jabbed a finger into her side which hurt!

Unease crept into Agnes' belly. What did he want from her?

"I understand, Uncle," she said in a small voice.

"And if you disagree with me again, I will remove you from here and make it so that your parents never allow you to leave Grinigoe again."

Agnes gasped. He was bent on keeping her under his thumb and she was sure if her parents knew they would never have allowed him to escort her. But she would not be coerced into doing anything that went against her nature. Whatever it was he was up to, she would not be a part of it.

They moved about the market and when Agnes stopped too long at a booth, her uncle nudged her to move on. By the end of the tour, she'd only bought a couple of items though she had desperately wanted to explore more.

She was also ever aware of the earl's presence behind them, as though he watched their every move. Did he suspect something? He would have to know she would never allow herself to be caught up in anything wicked. She didn't want anyone to think ill of her. But would they by association, if they thought her uncle could not be trusted?

The sun had set and tall torches lit the courtyard so bright it was as though the sun was still high in the sky. When the king and queen approached, the earl stepped toward her and offered his arm.

"My lady, would you kindly watch the fireworks display with me? I am certain your uncle will allow this simple delight and my assurance that you will be perfectly safe with me and Their Majesties."

Before her uncle could interrupt, she took his arm and said, "I would be honored, my lord. Thank you for your invitation."

"Sir, you are welcome to sit with the other gentry to the side of the courtyard within sight of us."

Thankfully her uncle did not protest and turned to stand with the rest of the crowd but not before he shot her a hard look that held all the promise of consequences. Bile rose in her throat. This was not a situation with which she was accustomed. She truly didn't know what she should do. Could she trust the earl? She didn't know him or anything about him. Nor did she know the queen well enough to unburden herself.

She would have to keep her wits about her around her uncle and around the earl for vastly different reasons.

When they were away from her uncle the earl said, "Are you unwell, Lady Agnes? It appears that something is troubling you."

Was he a mind reader? She'd been convinced earlier he'd stared into her soul, but had that given him access to her thoughts somehow?

"I am well, my lord, and thank you for offering to sit with me. My uncle does not offer stimulating conversation, and I fear does not easily converse with young women who are enamored with their first visit to court."

It wasn't a complete lie, but it was also far from the truth of the matter.

He smiled at her and her breath caught again. By God, he was a beautiful man with those unusual eyes and deep dimples on his tanned face. His teeth were perfectly straight, and he wore a light but neatly trimmed beard. His face was surely crafted by the angels.

They took their seats near the king and queen just before the first of the fireworks exploded in the sky above them. She jumped and a little squeal escaped from her before she could stop herself.

She knew what fireworks were but had never experienced them and she was in awe that something so beautiful had been dreamed up.

After a few explosions she noticed him staring at her again.

"Is aught amiss, my lord?" she asked with a sneaking suspicion he wanted to ask her something and she was keenly aware again of the silk chemise caressing her body.

"I am enjoying your company, Lady Agnes."

Convinced that was not at all what he wanted to say, she would accept it and turned her attention back to the festivities before her.

For the next couple of hours, she tried to enjoy herself and the small conversation passing between them, but kept seeing her uncle in the crowd glaring at her. She had no intention of being alone in his company at any point this evening so tried to devise a way to get to her chamber without him.

She didn't have to wait long.

From the side of the crowd, Fin walked directly toward her and offered his arm. "My lady, the queen bids you good evening and insists I escort you to your chamber. She has retired already and will see you at the morning meal in her apartment."

Agnes turned to the earl. "I thank you, my lord, for a lovely evening and for your company."

If he could read her mind, he would know that he'd in a way saved her from a terrible evening with her uncle or by herself in her chamber.

"You are most welcome, Lady Agnes. I will ensure your uncle finds his way to his chamber as well so you need not worry about him."

He *was* a mind reader!

Agnes took Fin's arm and curtseyed to the earl who offered a deep bow. With one last look at him, she turned and nearly bumped into Fin who was standing directly in front of her.

"I will escort my niece to her chamber."

Agnes jumped at his voice and held Fin's arm tighter when she felt a whoosh of air as the earl stepped around her and to Fin's side completely barring her from seeing her uncle.

"On her majesty the queen's orders, Fin will escort the lady to her chamber."

In a low voice that was just above a whisper, her uncle said, "She is not my queen."

The words were such a shock to her she was almost sure she had not heard them. A couple of finger snaps later and they were surrounded by the king's guard.

Agnes couldn't glean what was happening. One minute she was enjoying the company of the most enigmatic man she'd ever met and the next she was surrounded by guards and what? Would they throw her into the oubliette alongside her uncle? Those were his words and not how she felt at all. How did what was supposed to be her big adventure turn into such a mess?

"Fin, escort the lady to her chamber and post a guard outside." To one of the guards he said, "Detain this man until the king is ready to interrogate him. And have his chamber searched."

Without a glance in her direction or another word to her, he left the courtyard without a look back. When Fin finally turned to her, and she could see around him, her uncle was nowhere in sight.

"Are you well, Lady Agnes?"

"I—I do not know," she said. And she didn't know what to make of any of it.

"Come, my lady, I must see you securely to your chamber."

The jovial Fin from earlier was quiet and somber now and spoke no words to her as he opened the door for her to pass and then came the distinct click of the lock from the outside. She might not be detained like her uncle, but she was left in no doubt, she was not free to leave.

WITH JOHN SINCLAIR securely in a prison cell and heavily guarded, William and two guards searched his chamber. In his saddle bag they discovered missives to other Highland chiefs who believed as John had, that the current king did not deserve to sit upon the throne and that the rightful king was his father. William's heart sank when he read the words, *'We will right this wrong. Loyalty is everything!'*

The king had been right, and his intelligence had been sound. Now many questions emerged. Who were these others included in this plot? Was the king at risk alone or did they intend to share his fate with the queen? How much of this involved Lady Agnes?

He handed the missives to the guard. "Give these to the king and search the guest lists for any names included here. I don't care if they are third cousins twice removed, if any names on here are within these castle walls, the king will want them detained."

He was comfortable enough with the king's wishes to give these orders without question so from that chamber he went into his own. Nothing would happen this eve, so the best thing he could do now was to rest if he could and prepare for a long day tomorrow.

William stripped down to his trews and lay on top of the bed with his hands behind his head staring up at the canopy.

The king and his love for gatherings made it easy for anyone who was a threat to gain access to him and his family. Though there were many guards around, in the middle of a crowd with fireworks blazing, anyone could have been stealthy enough to harm them.

How long he lay there turning over scenarios in his mind, he did not know. After a time he drifted, but woke with a start to light stretching across the bed from the daybreak outside.

William sat up and stretched then reached for his leine and leather tunic. He splashed water on his face, wrapped his belt around his waist, and secured his blade. He prayed he would not need it, but he would not be caught without it.

Leaving the chamber, he noted how quiet and still everything was at this time of day before the world came to life and disrupted this blissful peace.

He made his way to the hall to see if any food had been

placed out yet and was pleased to find a few servants setting up and that there had been some platters of food from the previous night's feast freshly laid out for those early risers like himself.

Not far behind him was Fin who looked like he hadn't slept in a week offering to attend to William.

"You need not worry about me, Fin. I know you have a lot of responsibility here and I am quite capable of fending for myself. Beside which, you look like death warmed over. Did you not sleep?"

"I thank you, my lord. I attended to the king until the wee hours and insisted Archie rouse me the moment you were up."

"What has the king determined?"

"Of that I do not know, but he studied the missives for a long while and asked me to bring you to him as soon as you woke."

William needed to hear no more. He made his way to the king's solar and was immediately permitted entry. The king looked exhausted but sat up straight when William entered.

"Do you know two of the soon to arrive ladies in waiting are related to these documents and the plot to remove both myself and my queen from the throne?"

It was too much to take in. How coordinated they had been.

"Your Majesty, may I ask how you came to understand there was a plot in the first place?"

"Someone, whom I will protect with my life, from the Sinclair household sent me a message about a fortnight before I began planning this festivity."

"Someone who knew what John Sinclair and his niece were involved in?"

"Aye."

The king didn't deny her involvement, which was disappointing to William. He thought himself a fair judge of character and would have sworn she had no knowledge.

"So what happens now?"

"Now John Sinclair will remain in my holding cells until he is tried and judged."

"And his niece?"

William tried to ask the question in a nonchalant manner, but he was sure the king could read him well and that notion was verified when he smiled.

"Does it matter to you what happens to the lady?"

It did. He knew that with certainty in that moment.

"I would not want to see an innocent person tarred with the same brush with no evidence outside of association."

"And that makes you worthy of your title and my counsel, Montrose. I do not feel the lady is involved at the same level as her uncle, but I cannot see how, when in close proximity to him on the journey here, she would have no knowledge of his loyalties."

He made a fair point, and unless there were missives in her saddle bags, how would they ever know?

"What are your next steps for her?"

"I know her father will be on his way to collect her as soon as my message arrives. I will send riders and they will pass the message on so that he sees them as soon as possible. Until then, she will remain under guard in a chamber far from the queen."

"Do you suspect the earl's involvement?"

"I do not. I trust him as I do you. He is also a man who is worthy of his title."

So there was a chance Lady Agnes had the good sense of her father. There was one way he could find out for certain as he'd scarcely been able to remove her from his thoughts since first meeting her.

"Your Majesty, I would like to offer my services to remove Lady Agnes from here and return her to her father myself. That way she does not need to remain any longer than necessary and any potential danger is eliminated."

The king's eyes narrowed and he smiled. "Do I need to be concerned about a growing attachment to Lady Agnes, Montrose?"

The king was as shrewd as he'd ever been.

"Nay, Your Majesty. I merely offer my services to protect Your Majesties."

Leaning back in his chair, the king nodded. "Then I thank you and encourage you to keep your wits about you. I will send a message with my fastest riders to alert her father that she will be escorted by you and kept safe along the journey."

With that, William bowed to the king and retreated to the great hall in search of Fin. He found him to the side of the guest tables pointing a finger at Archie whose mouth was agape and looked positively mortified. The moment Fin noticed William approaching, he straightened and his expression changed from stern to completely masked.

"How can I assist, my lord?"

Before he could speak, Archie appeared to take advantage of the moment and scurried away. William had more pressing matters than to wonder about their quarrel, but he would make note of it.

"I plan to return Lady Agnes to her home in the north. The king agrees it is best if she return to her father, and I would like you to have the lady and her belongings collected and to meet me at the stables. The king has offered a comfortable carriage for her, and I will ride my horse together with six of his guards."

Fin's brow continued to lift as he took in the words. His mouth opened and closed a couple times but thankfully he didn't inundate William with a hundred questions. He left to do as he was bid, leaving William to look around the hall one more time before heading to the stable to secure the modes of transportation for the long journey north.

What would she think when Fin gave her the news? Would she be relieved? Shocked? Afraid? He certainly hoped it would not be the latter as he had no interest in frightening her, but maybe on the journey he could do what he intended to do all along: find out what she knew and how she was involved. God help him.

CHAPTER FIVE

S HE COULD HARDLY believe her ears. She would be sent home and escorted by the earl and her uncle would remain in Stirling prison.

"So they think I was in league with my uncle," she said to Fin who had been incredibly kind in sharing this information, but it was still difficult news to digest. Truth be told, she was sick to her stomach.

"They are erring on the side of caution to ensure the safety of the queen."

"Why does the earl need to escort me? Can I not remain in my chamber here until my father collects me?"

Fin shook his head. "Lady Agnes, it was the earl who volunteered to escort you."

"Why would he do that?"

He either didn't want to let her out of his sight because of his complete lack of trust in her, or—

"I do not know the earl's mind, Lady Agnes," Fin said interrupting her thoughts, "but I can speak for his integrity and loyalty."

Loyalty—that's what had gotten her into this mess in the first place. What would her parents say when she was returned so abruptly after what was supposed to be a triumphant entry into court? She was completely powerless in this situation and not even questioned before a judgment was made and sentence rendered. If only she'd listened closer to what her uncle had been telling her, she might have picked up on his intentions and could have shared that information, proving she was not a part of his schemes.

Too late for that now.

"I will have your chests brought to the stable, but you are to accompany me there now. The earl has secured one of the king's most comfortable carriages for you."

She could not be trusted, but she would be treated to her station. At least she could take comfort she would not return to her family in a prison cart.

Her shame would not be easily lifted, and she prayed her father would believe her. He had to! Her entire future hung in the balance of this business. Och, how she loathed her uncle for involving her in this.

Agnes watched as four manservants lifted her chests out of the chamber and four more came for the two filled with the gowns gifted by the queen. A maid packed the contents of the tall wardrobe.

"Fin, those aren't mine. You know I did not bring them."

"Aye, I know you did not bring them, and I also know the queen gifted you with them. You would not refuse the desire of your queen, now would you?"

She didn't quite know what to make of it. Did the queen think her innocent? She would go mad should she not understand what was happening soon.

Fin reached out to place his hand on her shoulder, then pulled it back and straightened himself. "All will be well, Lady Agnes. Come, we must make haste as I have to ensure the carriage is packed properly and there are sufficient provisions available to you for your journey."

She followed him through the hallway and down the stairs, noting there was not one other person about. Was that for their benefit or hers? Either way, she was grateful there were no prying eyes and gossiping members of the gentry about.

Even the stables were relatively empty save for one stable hand at the far end and some guards readying their horses. Was she to be escorted by them as well?

Fin opened the carriage door for her and helped her inside.

"I am hopeful I will see you again soon, Lady Agnes. Do take great care," he said and then placed his hand on his heart and bowed low. "It has been my great pleasure to meet you."

Before she could respond, he closed the door. From outside of the carriage, low male voices mumbled but she could not make out any specific words. Then one voice rang clear and her belly fluttered at the sound.

"Is aught secure?" The earl's voice was unmistakable, deep, and steady.

Agnes opened the curtain just for a peek and closed it again quickly when her eye caught his. This would be a torturous journey if they were to never converse. She wanted to tell him she was innocent but would not be so bold as to summon him. She must find a way to glean his thoughts on the matter.

When the carriage jolted a short time later, she realized he had no intention to speak with her at that moment. She sighed heavily and finally looked around the inside of the carriage. The seats were deep and lined with fine pale-green brocade. On one seat rested pillows and blankets and nearby a covered wooden basket with the butt of a loaf of bread poking out. These must be the provisions Fin had mentioned.

Fin. She sensed he had wanted to say so much more to her. She'd known him for such a short time but already was certain he was trustworthy.

Och, but she would go mad in this carriage with no one to converse for the next few days. Did they expect her to sleep here too? Was she to be hidden away not fit to be seen by anyone else? Well, by God she would not hide from anyone. Agnes pinned back the curtains and was pleased to discover a portion of the window could be opened and latched onto the side of the carriage from the inside. She did so on both sides and was pleased by the refreshing air moving through her space.

At least now she would not feel as though she were suffocating. Her chest was tight, only partly relieved by the fresh air.

Agnes peered through the window to see a large horse riding to the side of the carriage and upon inspection discovered the same on the other side. A few moments later someone cursed as the carriage halted with a jerk. She was thrown onto the bench across the carriage, air whooshing from her chest.

She was on her knees trying to recover herself when the door opened. Thankfully she landed on the pillows, but her knees would be bruised from hitting the floor so hard.

"Have a care, Lady Agnes," his deep voice warned.

"Me, have a care?" she asked incredulous when she had not known the carriage would stop like that. "I did not make the carriage stop so quickly." Her irritation with the whole situation had been building and this last incident was likely to make her blow. Polite address be damned.

Agnes composed herself and took her seat, smoothing out her skirts and keeping her eyes downcast. It was bad enough he'd come upon her in such a state. Must he patronize her as well?

"I am speaking of the windows. You must keep them closed."

"I will not keep them closed else I will be cooked like last eve's suckling pig!" She itched to cross her arms over her chest. Instead, she lifted her chin and met his gaze head on.

She would not stake her life on it, but it appeared one corner of his mouth lifted a little, before he drew his lips into a hard line.

"Lady Agnes, I do not wish for your discomfort, but it is imperative that you are not seen."

So she was right. They were keeping her hidden from sight. Was she to be treated like a leper?

"And why is that? I have not been offered sufficient explanation for any of this," she said sweeping her arm across the carriage.

"Fin has confirmed he shared information with you as I instructed."

"He told me the bare minimum, and you know that."

"There is much at stake and when we are successfully away from the city, I give you my word as a gentleman, you may ask as many questions as you like, and I will answer them all to the best of my ability."

She considered him for sincerity. His expression was unreadable, unfortunately, and since he held all the power in this situation, she would have to comply.

"Very well, my lord. But the windows remain open, I will unpin the curtains and that will conceal my identity but also provide the free flow of fresh air into the carriage."

His gaze roamed her face for a few moments before he nodded and closed the door. Not long after, the carriage lurched forward once again, and she contemplated what had just transpired. Was her concealment for her protection and if so from whom? Her uncle was in a prison cell, so he could not harm her. The king had set her up for the utmost of comfort and allowed additional guards along with a personal escort of the earl. Who might that leave? Did they think members of his court would be up in arms about the plot? That wasn't likely. Agnes was at a loss until she recalled her uncle referring to "we" a great deal in his stories. Maybe they weren't just stories, maybe he'd been telling her the plan all along. That meant there were other Highlanders out there who would want to be sure she didn't share any of their important plans. The sad reality was that she truly possessed no intelligence to impart.

Agnes sat back a little farther into the seat. She would heed the earl's warning and resist peeking through the windows.

THE LADY WAS infuriating in more ways than one. He could understand her perspective, but until he had time to question her thoroughly, he would be in charge of their journey. For all he knew, she could have ways to drop messages from the carriage. Perhaps this wasn't the best idea. But it was too late to second guess himself now. He would conceal her until they were well away from the city and then they could talk.

They rode for what felt like hours before he found lodgings where they could rest. He went inside and secured some rooms then returned to the carriage. When he opened the door, he found an open food basket in disarray and a soundly sleeping Lady Agnes.

In her slumber she looked so much at peace. She was an intriguing woman and under different circumstances, he would be interested in knowing her more. But he could not let his growing interest in her cloud his judgment in this matter. There was too much riding on the truth.

William placed his hand on her shoulder and gave her a little nudge. Her eyes fluttered open and for a moment she blinked slowly as if she couldn't place herself. She looked around the carriage then sat up rubbing her eyes.

"Where are we?" she asked and covered mouth with her hand as she yawned.

"We are in a wee village called Balquhidder and I have secured rooms for us for the evening. No one will think to look for us here."

Her expression transformed from peaceful sleepiness to something sharper as her brows drew tight and she frowned. It was as though she'd just recalled the events that placed her there.

"Come inside, Lady Agnes, and let us break a meal together. I know you have many questions, as do I."

He held out his hand to assist her and after careful inspection of both his hand and his face, she took it and stepped out onto the ground. He had no intention of letting go of her hand unless she wanted him to so he held it to see what she would do. It felt right somehow, her tiny hand in his.

They entered the inn and took a table by the hearth. William was well aware of this place as he'd passed through many times in his travels. The owner came straight over to them with a pot of something that bubbled and smelled delicious. He couldn't tell just how much of the basket Lady Agnes had sampled, but he'd not eaten anything since earlier that morn before leaving Stirling, only stopping when the lady required privacy. By now he was ravenous.

He waited until she began her meal then he dug into his own. He had to approach his questions carefully and realized he would likely tell much from those asked of him. What was she most concerned about?

They sat in silence as they shared their meal with tension growing as thick as the stew. He had to change the tone else they would get nowhere.

"Are you comfortable in the carriage, Lady Agnes? Do you have everything you require?"

"Aye, my lord. 'Tis quite luxurious and nothing like the one that brought me here."

"I am ready for your questions now, if you like," he said, hoping they could remain civil to one another during the exchange. For whatever it was, he did not like to see a frown upon her lovely face.

"I thank you, my lord. My first question is why is my uncle detained?"

Did he tell here everything or the bare minimum? Was she asking that just to glean how much they knew? At some point he would have to make a leap of faith and now was as good a time as any.

"Your uncle carried missives from other men in the Highlands who sought to bring harm upon the royal family."

Agnes's eyes grew wide as she dropped her bread into the remaining stew in her bowl. She sat back staring at him.

"Were you aware of these missives?" he asked.

"My lord, obviously not. What else did they contain?"

"Commitments of the houses to join the cause to unroot the

false king and to offer ladies to attend the queen."

The lady gasped openly then and her cheeks flamed. "The queen?" she whispered.

"Aye, Lady Agnes, the queen is also at risk."

"So why am I not imprisoned? Or at least put in a cell. I am well aware I am not free at the moment."

"Because I wanted to speak with you myself to determine the extent of your involvement. Detaining you at Stirling Castle where you could access the queen until your father collected you was not the best option."

"And that is why you volunteered to escort me. So you could interrogate me yourself. Go ahead then," she said and folded her arms across her chest, "ask me your questions."

And there was the tension rising again. But they were in it now and it was just as well to barrel ahead while she was talking to him.

"Very well. Lady Agnes, you say you were not aware of the missives, but did your uncle engage you to be a part of this plot?"

She unfolded her arms and placed her hands in her lap, lowering her head. "I believe he was trying to."

"What do you mean by trying to?"

Lady Agnes drew in a deep breath. "He told me of many histories along our journey, but I confess, I found them to be boring and so only pretended to listen."

She peeked up at him, and he was so relieved by her confession he couldn't help but smile at her. She smiled slowly at him then as well. It was the first time since he'd arrived at Stirling Castle and was informed of the threat that he had any inkling that all would be well.

"May I ask where your thoughts were focused?" he asked a little softer than his earlier questions. He could see her emotions on her face as her demeanor turned from defensive to more shy embarrassment.

"I know 'tis disrespectful to him, but truly I had no interest in events of long ago and I was excited to see the castle and meet the queen for the first time and—" she stopped abruptly and looked down.

"And what else, Lady Agnes?"

She lifted her gaze to him then and tilted her chin up slightly. "If you must know, my lord, I was looking forward to meeting the lords and ladies of the court and hoping I might meet someone I would fancy. And there is nothing wrong with that."

William had to hide a chuckle. Nothing wrong indeed. She was every bit the innocent lady she should be with her thoughts tightly tied to her own wishes.

He leaned back and let out a sigh. He was pleased with her confession beyond measure, and he was now convinced she had not willingly been a part of Sinclair's plan. He would send word back to the king immediately and tomorrow if she wanted to take the top off the carriage, she could fill her boots.

"There is nothing wrong with that at all, Lady Agnes. I would expect exactly that from a lady new to court."

"Is it only you who thinks me involved with my uncle?"

The question hit hard. They had all assumed the worst of her before questioning her and that didn't sit well with him. He was not normally the sort of man who judged too quickly, yet he'd done just that with her.

"I do not think you were involved at all, and I know the queen and Fin insisted upon your innocence as well."

"But you did, as did the king, else I would not have been banished."

She had a point, but there was little they could do about it now. She would have to accept what had occurred and that they now believed her.

"I am convinced, and that will be enough for the king."

"And this could have been cleared up last night in a quick conversation, yet here we are on the road to my home, and my reputation will be affected."

He hadn't thought of that aspect as the monarch's safety had been more important than anything in the heat of the moment.

"Your reputation will not be affected with the favor of the king and queen behind you."

"And yet, I am still destined for home." She pushed back her chair and said, "I am travel weary, my lord. Which chamber is mine?"

"Top of the stairs, first on the right. I bid you good night, Lady Agnes."

She nodded lightly and turned to retreat to her chamber. Moments later, a door slammed and though he could not hear it, he was sure a lock clicked right after. He'd certainly made a mess of that, but at least the ice was now broken.

CHAPTER SIX

L EANING AGAINST THE door after she locked it offered the first moment of peace since she'd left her home. And while she was pleased the earl believed her, she was not pleased with his lack of respect for her reputation when taking action that could absolutely be perceived by her peers that she'd been involved. Word would spread. It always did. Then she'd be hard pressed to ever attend court again.

Agnes pulled away from the door and clawed at the ties of her gown to remove the garments as quickly as possible. A small satchel had been brought up from the carriage, and she was grateful to see her linen night shift inside versus the traitorous silk one given to her by the queen.

And about the queen. The woman had the good sense to know Agnes would not be a part of such a foolish plot, as did Fin! Her two friends had been true to her, but not the lofty "men" who had to protect security at all costs and let common sense fly out the window. Who was hurt most in this scenario? The answer was obvious to her but not to them.

Once home she would write to the queen and thank her for her support and ask her to thank Fin as well. She would not let their actions alter her plan to have control over her future marriage either.

She had many days left to travel with the earl so she would

want to find a way to get along but she was just so vexed with him at the moment. Och, and to think she'd been so enamored at first. True, she still considered him to be the handsomest man in all of Scotland with those damned unusual eyes that changed color in every light. Below stairs earlier had been the worst with the firelight dancing in them and turning them the color of wheat at harvest. No, she wouldn't focus on his godlike visage, or his broad shoulders. He could keep it all. She would forget all about the Earl of Montrose as someone she wanted to know better and focus her attention elsewhere. She didn't want to be a countess anyway. She would be perfectly happy in a nice country manor by the sea with a good honest husband and lots of wee bairns to love.

And maybe if she kept telling herself that, it might help eliminate the onslaught of images of him crossing her mind day and night.

Agnes prepared herself for bed and just as she turned back the sheets she noticed the latch wiggle at her door. A single sound not quite like a knock was followed by a whispered *"I'm sorry"* then heavy footfalls that went down the hall. A door opened then closed.

She stared at the door for long moments before turning her attention back to the bed. Though she wore her linen shift, the sensation of the silk washed over her body. Her nipples hardened and moisture pooled between her legs. Agnes squeezed her eyes tight to conjure anything else that would take him from her mind. But neither the image of a violent storm nor of Bregdi itself could shake the feeling of knowing he was in the chamber next to hers.

Was he in bed already? What would it feel like to have his strong arms around her now assuring her all would be well. She shook her head and pulled the covers up as high as she possibly could. No! She would not allow unladylike thoughts about a man who had displayed such a lack of trust in her. She would not and could not.

Agnes tossed and turned for much of the night until she finally found slumber. In it, her dreams were as troubling as when she was awake.

She was chased through Stirling Castle by an unknown threat and voices just around corners only to find no one there. A voice behind her told her he was sorry as he placed his hand on her shoulder. When she turned, he was gone. Back and forth the dream tormented her as fear warred with desire.

She woke with a start to a light knocking on her door. Flinging back the covers she stood by the door to see if it was real or part of her dream.

"Lady Agnes, are you unwell?" His voice was soft and full of concern.

"I—I am well, my lord," she said. "I had a bad dream."

"Do you wish me to watch over you?"

Och, that wasn't a good idea considering the turn of her thoughts earlier. Yet she found herself turning the latch to allow him entry. The sight of him quickened her pulse. He was bare chested with his trews not fully buttoned. His hair which was usually neatly tied at his nape was down around his shoulders and his eyes, those damned eyes trailed the length of her. It was then she realized the state of her own undress.

She should have slammed the door and locked it immediately. So why didn't she? Because she didn't want to. She reveled in the sensations flowing through her body just by looking at him. She was aware of the happenings between a husband and wife but didn't know those feelings could be invoked so easily without a single touch.

"Do you?"

Did she what? Want him to caress her like her silk shift? Aye, very much so, but she was not about to tell him that.

"Lady Agnes you must say something or—" his voice broke off in a whisper.

Or what she was gleaning and understanding. His body was tense as his hands grasped the door frame drawing attention to his thickly muscled chest. She'd never seen a man in such a state of undress, and she couldn't help but let her eyes wander the length of him. A light dusting of hair splayed across his chest and trailed down across his rigid belly to disappear inside his trews. In the dark she could not see anything more, but his breathing changed.

"Lady Agnes, you cannot look at me like that," he whispered.

Still, she could not stop herself from doing just that. By the stars, whoever made him had sculpted him from the gods.

Finally, his words sank in and she understood. He felt the same rush she did and the danger of the situation hit home.

"I am well, my lord, and do not require assistance," she said shutting the door and turning the lock which made a loud click. The sound was enough to bring her fully into the present.

Agnes jumped back into bed, hugging her knees and rocking. Oh aye, she was in more trouble with that man than she had previously thought. She'd have to keep a sensible distance from him lest she find herself in far worse ruin than being banished from the king's court.

She was sure she would gain no more slumber this night and so pulled a chair over to the dying embers of the hearth. She placed a few more small pieces of wood on the fire and stared into its flames as though it would reveal her future.

To no avail.

Agnes curled up into a ball on the chair and leaned her head back. She would find a way for all to be well. She longed for her parents' counsel. Until then, she would have to trust her own judgment and keep the irresistible earl at arm's length.

WILLIAM DREW IN a shaky breath and made his way back to his room. Once inside he closed the door and crawled into bed. His cock was hard as a rock and his body was filled with a level of desire he'd never encountered. The image of her with the pale moonlight highlighting the silhouette of her curvaceous body nearly drove him mad with need for her. He would never take advantage of a situation or do anything without her full agreement, but by God, he wanted her more than he ever thought possible. He'd been aroused before, plenty of times, and found his release in many pleasing ways. But this woman brought out something new in him. He hungered for her, craved her touch.

Christ's teeth, how would he survive several more days in her presence without acting like a lad who had never learned the ways between men and women?

William removed his trews and tossed them across the room. He hopped out of bed as though it contained burning embers and stood by the open window, willing the cool night air to still the molten heat flowing through him. He'd recognized her beauty the moment he first saw her, but beauty meant nothing if the woman did not possess a genuine spirit and sense of herself. Agnes had shown herself to be curious and kind with all the noble attributes he'd always desired.

While there was nothing he could do to change the events leading them to this moment, he could ensure he took the steps he needed to protect her going forward. Whether she was meant for him or not, she'd proven herself worthy of her station and loyal to the crown and he would see to it the entirety of the king's court felt the same way.

For now, he would treat her with the respect her father would expect for her. He'd only met the Earl of Caithness once and upon that meeting had gleaned a favorable impression of the man's integrity. It appeared he had imparted that good trait upon his daughter.

As William's logic formed, his body cooled to the point he could stand the sensation of the bedding on his skin. Climbing back into bed, he stared up at the ceiling and formed a plan for the next day. He hoped she liked it.

William woke at daybreak as he always had. For the first few moments, he forgot where he was and thought about what he would do that day with his family and how he could help his tenants, and then he remembered. He wasn't a long way from his home, but he would likely not see it for a few weeks yet.

Tossing back the covers, he sat up in bed and swiped his hands down across his face. Did the lady even like riding horseback? He didn't know, but he was about to find out. Something in him was certain she'd approve.

He dressed quickly and descended the stairs two at a time. His mood was light at the thought of doing something pleasing for her.

Outside, and around the back of the inn, he found the owner and enquired about purchasing a well-tempered mare. Within half an hour, the deal was struck and he was in possession of a beautiful young silver-gray mare fit with a lady's saddle.

He'd requested a full early morning feast for Lady Agnes and himself along with the six guardsmen who looked like they'd enjoyed their evening in the village and could use the sustenance. The grateful men attacked the feast as soon as it was put before them.

Now only one thing remained. He paused at her door and drew in a deep breath, squared his shoulders, and knocked.

The door opened almost immediately. She was fully dressed and her hair was pinned back, unlike her normal flowing tresses, and her expression was cool and masked. He gave her a broad smile. She had no idea of his intent and was on guard. And rightly so.

"Lady Agnes, if it is your wish, I would like you to join me to break our fast below. The cook has prepared some delectable offerings for us including cold smoked arctic char and salmon."

Her brows drew close together for a moment.

"I would suspect you are hungry?"

After a few moments she said, "Aye, I would like that very much, my lord." She moved past him toward the stairs leaving her belongings inside.

This gave him a wee spark of encouragement. He would have her bags brought down and she would continue along the journey with him. It wasn't a stretch of logic. If she was bent on finding her own way, she would be holding her bags in her hand.

Once seated and with the spread of smoked fish and steaming bread before them, Lady Agnes appeared to lose some of the rigidity displayed moments ago. It was a good meal he'd sampled many times before. Loch Voil yielded perfect fish for smoking, and the owner knew his way around presentation.

"I have a surprise for you," he said and enjoyed the way her gaze locked with his immediately.

It was clear she tried to mask her interest, but she was not skilled at hiding her true emotions. He was beginning to admire that about her.

"Is your interest not piqued?" he asked.

"It is, my lord. But I confess, given the circumstances, it is unexpected."

Point conceded. He would have to change tactics.

"Given the circumstances, it is an offering of good faith."

She tilted her head to the side. "Good faith, you say, my lord."

"Aye, Lady Agnes. And the longer you idle about your meal, the longer before you discover it."

He leaned back in his chair and topped pieces of bread with the irresistible smoked fish and popped bits into his mouth as he watched this graceful lady battle poise with hunger and curiosity.

When she was finished, she lightly dabbed her mouth with the cloth provided and stared at him intently.

"Well done, Lady Agnes. Are you ready for your surprise?"

In a voice he was certain was forced and tempered, she said, "Aye, my lord. If you wish to show me this surprise now, I am ready for it."

It was a small victory, but one nonetheless.

Pushing back his chair, William stood and reached out his hand to the lady. She accepted and together they stepped outside.

Her gasp was audible and she quickly turned to him.

"Is this for me?"

His heart picked up a few beats in that moment. He had no idea how much pleasing her would bring to his own satisfaction and delight.

"Aye, Lady Agnes. She is yours now and you must give her a proper name. You may ride her as much as you like during our journey and she will be cared for each eve by the guards as they care for the other horses."

She turned to him with a smile and tears in her eyes. "I thank you, my lord, for she is the most beautiful creature I have ever beheld. I would very much like to ride for as long as I am able each day."

William hoisted her atop the mare and ensured she was secure. He held the reins and gazed up at the joy on her face.

"Right," he said as he turned to mount his own horse and begin the day's journey.

They rode for many hours with appropriate stops along the way. Every time he caught her attention he read pure pleasure on her expression. Her smile was infectious.

Riding alongside her after a time, he asked, "Have you given her a name, Lady Agnes?"

"Aye, my lord, I have," she said with a grin. "She will be known as Catriona as she is as pure of heart of any creature I've ever known." As she said this, she stroked the mare's neck. The mare bobbed its head up and down. "Truly she is a great gift, and I do not know how to thank you."

The genuine light surrounding her was gift enough. Maybe this one small gesture was a start on how he might bridge the distance between them.

"I am pleased you like her," he said. "I understood you did not want to be secluded in the carriage during our journey. And now we are away from the city and the most danger to you, I believe it is safe."

She brought it up then. "You still fear for my safety?"

"Aye, Lady Agnes." How could she not see the inherent danger? "We do not know the extent to which your uncle and those in his element have infiltrated these roads."

With that she looked around them, promptly dismounted, and strode toward the carriage.

"Lady Agnes, you are safe with me here riding beside you."

"Am I? You admit it, you don't know how many of the houses in those missives merely responded or took action. We will ride through many of their lands, that much I remember from my uncle's ramblings. As much as I appreciate your gift, I will take my chances with the heat and the midges in the carriage."

She entered the carriage and slammed the door. William took Catriona's reins and secured them to the back of the carriage and signaled for the group to continue forward.

Christ, could he not gain an inch with her? He thought he'd done a kind service for her, but here he was again losing favor.

William shook his head and kicked his heels into his horse's side. He'd ride ahead for a bit to clear his head. This lady was proving to be more of a challenge than he'd anticipated. Maybe, his whole approach was not so well crafted after all.

CHAPTER SEVEN

S ITTING IN THE carriage alone and stewing over the earl was ridiculous. She was getting on her own nerves now. But she had to make a point. Was she in danger or not? She did recall some of the names; there were Grant, Ross, and Munroe names on that list and they would pass through each of their lands in order. And she didn't want to spend the next several days cooped up in a carriage no matter how luxurious.

After about an hour and once she settled herself, she tapped on the carriage roof. It came to a stop almost immediately.

She didn't wait for the door to be opened for her, rather opened it and hopped out, nearly tripping on her skirts. She straightened and smoothed her skirt.

The earl trotted to her but said nothing. So she lifted her chin and said, "My lord, I should like to ride Catriona. Will you help me mount her?"

His mouth opened slightly with a curl, and then he closed it. He dismounted and untied her horse from the back of the carriage and then reached out his hand to her. She took it and then strong hands encircled her waist. The pressure as his hands tightened when he lifted her sent wicked sensations through her.

Her breath caught in her throat once she was above him and caught him staring at her with a peculiar expression. It wasn't quite anger, certain not joviality, but his eyes darkened as he continued to stare at her. Her gaze flicked down to his mouth which was parted slightly and his lips curled into a faint smile.

"Are you seated well, Lady Agnes?"

His voice was like silk on her skin. She shivered for a moment wondering what that voice would be like in her ear. She shook the thought away. This was getting out of control.

Shifting on the saddle, she positioned herself for comfort, held the reins and horn, and nodded. "Aye, my lord, I am well seated and ready."

With one more glance toward him she turned her thoughts from the vision of him with his honey-colored eyes, and broad, leather-clad shoulders and thick chest, and urged Catriona forward.

Freedom. That was what riding on her own horse meant to her. To be fully in the capacity to direct her movements was liberating, even if only in this small way. Her parents had controlled sending her to Stirling, her uncle had controlled her time at the castle, and now the earl controlled the result of her uncle's scheming. She was irritated with the lot of them, but she could have this one piece of independence, and she would take full advantage.

The earl, to his credit, did not force her from her horse or tell her when she would need to rest. She determined each time she needed to rest and relieve herself. He for the most part left her alone, so she took in the beautiful country around her.

Flat plains gave way to rocky cliffs and pops of heather on the mountains in the distance. They galloped along the edge of Loch Ness, and she grinned to herself about the stories she'd been told about the most famous monster in all of Scotland. Och, she was sure her Bregdi could give that old Loch Ness monster a run for its money.

Her days were filled with living in the moment of enjoying the beautiful countryside and her nights were filled with increasingly vivid dreams of the man who mostly rode quietly beside her. He appeared to be lost amongst his own thoughts, so she carried on lost in her own.

On the morning of the day they were to arrive at Inverness, he lingered a little longer after hoisting her atop Catriona. After, he mounted his horse and rode alongside her.

"My lord, is aught amiss?"

He blinked a couple of times and said, "You have surprised me, Lady Agnes."

She had? "How so, my lord?"

"You have ridden for days on end and with no complaint. I do not know any other lady who would have done so."

"It is the only freedom I have, my lord. I did not choose this path."

He paused for a moment. "I know you have not. And you have not ranted or portrayed victim of your circumstance. I have noticed you staring off about the countryside and smiling."

His quiet contemplation had clearly been about her, at least for part of the time, and she hadn't realized.

"I have been recounting some of the stories I have been told over the years about the legends around this part of the country."

"Which ones?" he asked appearing genuinely interested.

"I wondered if the sea creature of Loch Ness would win in a battle with our Bregdi."

When he smiled and his dimples appeared, she was trans-fixed. He had an air of power about him, but he did not abuse it. She'd seen plenty of other people puff themselves up because of their title undeservedly, and even in her uncle's case do the same without the title.

But this man was different. He'd not badgered her to see his side of the situation over the past days, rather, kept watch over her, but did not try to interfere with her. She admired him for that.

"We have some legends of our own at Mugdock Castle," he said. "Would you like to hear about them?"

"Aye, my lord, I would very much."

He told her of a gray lady who roamed the halls of the castle in search of her lost bairn. "Mugdock Castle is built on the ruin of a much older place, said to have existed long before the Gaels moved here and farmed the land for their own."

"Have you seen her?"

"Aye, that I have when I was a wee lad myself."

"Tell me about it, please," she said and shifted a little so she could see him better.

"I was about seven or eight summers and had been sent to my chamber for stealing sweet buns from the kitchen."

She could almost envision this beautiful wee lad with a mop of curly brown hair being scolded by the cook.

"Were ye not stealthy as a lad then, my lord?"

"I held my own. Are you saying you were never caught taking something you wanted?"

"Aye, I am saying just that. I would be in and out of that kitchen before the cook could turn around. I'm saying I'm stealthy and quick," she said with a smile.

His smile mirrored her own and she realized they were staring at one another again. Not that she minded, but one moment they could be arguing and the other like this.

"And so you were sent to your chamber hopefully with your sweet bun."

"Alas, that was confiscated, but aye, I was on my way to accept my punishment when I saw a shadowy image walking toward me. The hallway leading to the children's chambers was long and so I was on one end and this figure approached from the opposite end."

"What did you do?"

"I did what any young lad would do. I froze," he said and laughed. "The hair stood on the back of my neck as I watched this thing come toward me, seeming to look straight at me and just before it reached me, it disappeared."

"My lord, did you tell anyone?"

"I believe I would like you to call me William when 'tis just us, Lady Agnes."

His words were unexpected. That privilege was reserved for those betrothed or married and they were neither. But she would confess to herself, she'd wanted to call him by his given name since the moment she met him.

"Very well, William. And I believe you are trying to change the subject."

His smile disappeared when she said his name but returned with her accusation.

"That was it, that was the end of the story."

"I do not believe you told no one."

"It is the truth. You are the first person I have ever shared my encounter with the Gray Lady."

The whole conversation had become so personal and intimate she wasn't quite sure what to make of it.

"Then I thank you for sharing it with me," she said.

"Did it meet your standards for unusual creatures?" he asked with one brow cocked.

It took her a moment to realize what he was saying. "Och! You fibbed! You have never seen a ghost," she said and couldn't help but laugh at the way he now sat straighter in his saddle and brushed invisible dust from his arms.

He then placed his arm across his chest and bowed. One thing was for sure: he had an infectious sense of humor she'd not expected. Aye, upon closer inspection, there was much more to this man than she'd ever imagined. She would need to be mindful, lest she find herself at risk of letting her feelings get the best of her and making a complete and utter arse of herself.

WILLIAM LOVED THE banter between them. He'd been considering her over the past few days, watching the various expressions cross her lovely face, as though she were having complete conversations internally. He'd come to the realization he wanted to be part of them and know what could make her smile so freely or draw her brows together while staring off at a distant mountain. For some unaccountable reason, he wanted to be a part of her sphere.

Truth be told, he'd never been one to sneak sweets from the kitchen. He preferred to use charm to fill his belly with delicious creations by one kitchen hand in particular who could not resist his compliments. By the time he was twelve, she would automatically set some aside for him.

Agnes had not invited him to address her informally as he had, but he would wait to see if she did. The sound of his name on her lips was pleasing. Those lips. The ones he'd begun dreaming about every night that he wanted to taste. Her neck he wanted to kiss. Her body he wanted to caress and pleasure. Aye, he was already in it too deep for his liking, but he was powerless to fight the rushing desire she instilled in him whenever he thought of her.

Each night he would pleasure her until neither could stand it any longer, only to wake in the morning alone and unsatisfied.

But she was a lady.

And as a lady, she was not available unless he was ready to make that kind of commitment to her and her family.

He'd considered that a great deal over the past days riding quietly behind her. There was no barrier, only his desires and hers. And so here he was, doing his best to find out just that. But he wasn't fooling anyone, least of all himself. He'd known he wanted to make her his the moment she entered the great hall at Stirling Castle.

And now he would also discover her wishes. She'd been embarrassed to speak of her desires to find a husband, and understandably so. Young ladies did not normally speak of such things to unattached men as it could be seen as unbecoming and desperate. But she was not like that and the sentiment she'd shared was not in that context.

Now before him, he considered this bright, beautiful woman

with a striking imagination and a kind soul. Fin had seen it immediately and had voiced his concern in the most authoritative way possible for a man of his station. He'd practically threatened harm to William should one hair on her head be out of place upon her arrival at her home.

William grinned thinking about the disheveled state she'd be in if he could have the kind of night with her he longed for.

"Are you plotting your next fairytale, William, or remembering something pleasurable."

Christ, even the way she said pleasure made his loins react.

"I was indeed thinking of pleasurable things, Lady Agnes," he said in a pointedly low voice.

She shifted in her saddle, and he hoped it was for the reasons his mind conjured.

"I suppose, William, since I am to address you by your given name when there is no one else around, that you may do the same."

"Thank you, Agnes. You do me quite the honor."

Tilting her head to the side, she asked, "May I ask what color are your eyes? I can never quite make it out."

He pulled back on the reins and stopped his horse and waited until she did the same. If that wasn't an invitation, he didn't know what was.

"Would you like to take a closer look?"

She turned her head toward him as he leaned down closer to her. Their horses were side by side allowing him to hold his face just inches from hers. He had full control over his horse to remain steady, and he would with hers as well if need be.

This moment would tell him everything he needed to know about her desires, and he was already well on his way to knowing the truth of it as her breathing became ragged.

"Agnes," he whispered. "You are so beautiful."

"I—"

"May I kiss you?"

She swallowed hard and in a small voice said, "Aye."

He brushed his lips across hers as he reached one hand up to stroke the tender skin below her ear. He then held the back of her neck and drew her into a deeper kiss, parting her lips and tasting her sweetness. When she returned the kiss matching his movements, he sought her tongue. By God, she must be an enchantress come to drive him mad with desire.

When their tongues met and danced, she groaned in her throat. It was too much. He could not lay a finger on her and then not have her. He pulled back and stared hard into her eyes. There was more desire there than he'd ever seen in a woman's eyes before.

"Agnes," he whispered again. "I cannot resist you. I want you so badly. Forgive me, but I cannot kiss you like that again. It is too powerful, and I will not be able to stop from pleasuring you until you scream my name and beg for release."

He was well aware how he sounded, but he couldn't do this to himself or to her. She was a lady and as such deserved to be treated with respect and protected. Not taken advantage of on a deserted road with no one to intercept and intervene. He was her protecter. Who would save her from him?

Ages straightened up and touched her lips. "But what if I want you to kiss me?"

"You cannot say that, Agnes. I only have so much self-control."

Did she not understand what was at stake?

After a few moments, she pulled away from him, adjusted herself, and trotted ahead. He sat back and raked his hand through his hair then scraped his hand down across his face. Christ's teeth, he'd made a mess of it. Just when he had broken through and gotten onto common ground with her, he had to take it to a level from which they could not return. What was done could not be undone.

William rode behind her and matched her speed when she wanted to gallop and when she wanted to trot. Thankfully the guards had been keeping a good distance ahead and behind them and would not have seen anything.

They rode in silence for the remainder of the journey to Inverness. He'd had a long-running understanding with the Gordon of Inverness Castle, that he would find lodgings there at any time required or desired. The same arrangement was reciprocated as both clans were well favored with one another.

By his estimation, they would reach the castle before sundown, and from there they would break a meal together. Then they would not have to see one another again until the next day. He would give her all the space she desired, but he would know her whereabouts at all times. He'd promised to protect her, and that's exactly what he intended to do, even if it meant keeping her at arm's length.

Or…

He could do the right thing and ask for her hand. There had never been, and would never be another woman he desired more, so why did he hesitate? He could think of no good reason. And once he'd come to that realization, his entire outlook changed. He could see them at Mugdock Castle, loving one another and raising a family together. She would be the addition he'd always dreamed of. The more he thought of it, the lighter his heart lifted than it had been for a long time.

Now he needed to formulate a plan and explore the perfect moment to execute it. He would ask her, but he couldn't formally announce anything until he spoke with her father. There needn't be any reason for anyone to question propriety on either of their part.

Aye, he would make her his. Every part of that made him want to gallop up to her, lift her onto his saddle, and never let her go again. He decided he would do at least the first part and took off to catch up with her. Once she realized he was galloping hard toward her, she took off and it was a while before he actually caught up. By the time he did, she'd slowed to a trot and frowned.

"Have you gone mad in the head?" she asked.

"I have finally found clarity, Agnes."

"Then I suggest you use it to fuel your common sense. You could have spooked her and harmed me."

Put like that, he did realize he was a wee bit overzealous, but he couldn't help himself. He smiled broadly at her, "I do apologize, my lady. I did not mean to spook your horse or startle you. I had a sudden need to be near you."

She shook her head and turned back to look at the road ahead. From his vantage point, he was intently aware of a small smile resting on her lips. And he intended to keep it there.

CHAPTER EIGHT

T HE MAN HAD clearly lost his wits. And the range of emotions over the past few hours were inexplicable. She much preferred the smiling, lighthearted William who rode alongside her now to the brooding one from earlier. What had brought about all these changes in him she could not say as she had been exploring her own thoughts and feelings.

The kiss had been anticipated but nothing could have prepared her for the feelings he'd stirred in her. She'd felt desire for him, but this was so much more. No silk shift could produce this tingling and ache from deep within her as though she craved something she did not yet understand, leaving her unfulfilled and wanting more.

When they finally arrived at Inverness Castle, she was glad for the brief reprieve to be attended on in her chamber but found herself feeling empty without his nearness. So much so that when a knock sounded at the door signaling the evening meal, she practically leapt at it.

On the other side was a neatly trimmed and well put together William holding out a single bluebell for her.

She'd opted to change into her favorite plain blue velvet gown which was more comfortable than the complicated gowns gifted her by the queen. This one was squared off around her neckline with long floor-length sleeves that were fitted to her elbow and then cascaded downward. She debated between her linen shift and the silk one and in the last minute decided on the latter. She hoped the garment would not prove too distracting.

He on the other hand seemed dressed to perfection with his hair pulled back and tied at his nape wearing his shiny black tunic, perfectly set over a fresh white leine. He wore leather trews and tall boots with his clan's sash across his chest. She felt far less formal.

"Are we dining with the king and queen this eve, my lord?" she said with a smile only partly jesting.

"Nay, my lady. But we do have cause to celebrate."

"Do we now?"

"Aye."

"And what are we celebrating?" she asked taking his arm as they strolled through the hallway toward the great hall.

"You shall see," he said and placed his hand atop hers giving her a little squeeze.

Any part of him that touched her sent shivers racing through her body. She became aware of the heat and strength in his hand and now regretted the silk. She would not survive this night without wanting to straddle him and kiss him until they were both breathless.

When they entered the hall, her breath caught. The table had been adorned with bunches of fresh flowers and tall candles with dancing flames. The hearth with its ornately decorated stonework depicted a stag head staring hard out from within as though the beast had gotten caught inside while trying to escape.

The walls were covered with various tapestries depicting battles and more stag's heads than she'd ever seen. The table was set for two at the far end. She looked up to William to find him grinning down at her.

"Is all this for me?"

"Aye, Agnes. Will you enjoy a meal with me?"

She answered by moving to the chair she assumed was meant for her which was to the side of the head of the table.

William helped her onto her seat just as servants entered with platters of fish and rabbit and boar. Bread platters followed by pastry and cheese taking up about a quarter of the table.

"Are all the king's guard joining us?"

He laughed. "No, it is just us. The family are away and the servants are under strict orders to treat us well. The Gordon and I go back a long way. Standing orders at Mugdock Castle as well."

"A little warning would have helped, my lord. I feel under-dressed for this elaborate display," she said as she pointed at some perfectly prepared trout when prompted by a servant. The fish was complemented by cheese, bread, and a savory blueberry duff. The meal was fit for a king, but she'd happily take it. She was not accustomed to feasts like these as an everyday occurrence.

"Would you prefer ale or mead?" he asked.

"Mead, please. If I drink ale with this food, I will be asleep on my trencher." It was true she did not prefer ale and even mead only on occasion. She much preferred the light wines her father had brought over from France on a regular basis. The other beverages were much heavier than her liking.

Once the meal was finished, he asked, "Would you like to sit by the fire with me, Agnes?"

She noticed a comfortable bench had been brought in that wasn't there when they'd entered.

"I would enjoy that, William."

He pulled back her chair and reached out his hand to her. She placed hers in his and together they sat on the thickly padded wide bench facing the hearth. The fire wasn't overly large considering the warm summer weather, but it did keep the air from gaining a chill from the stone walls. The ambience was comforting.

Everything about the evening had been perfect. And how here she sat, with the handsome earl and no place in the world she would rather be.

"May I ask you something?"

"Aye, William, you can ask me anything."

"Earlier today, when I kissed you," he said.

Her belly fluttered and her pulse quickened at the mere mention.

"Aye?"

"Did you enjoy it?"

She searched his expression for any hint of condescension or jest, but there was none.

"Aye," she whispered. "I did."

"Would you let me kiss you again?"

He'd said 'twas too dangerous. And he'd been right. She was an earl's daughter and meant for a great marriage. She could not give herself over to her desires, just because a man was handsome and a damned fine kisser.

"William, you said earlier that wasn't a good idea. Have you changed your mind?"

She was aware she'd worded that awkwardly. Did she want to kiss him? Aye, that and more, but she had to be sensible about it. She had a real sense of where it would lead.

"Something has changed, aye."

"Tell me what has changed."

He leaned toward her and stroked her cheek with his thumb. "By God, no one has ever captivated me the way you have."

That wasn't new; he'd told her that before.

William cupped her face with his hands and touched his nose with hers before holding his lips inches from hers. "Tell me you are as stirred as I am," he whispered.

There was no doubt about it. "I am."

"Tell me you want me as much as I want you."

"I do."

Her brain would not let her form more flowery words than the simple truth and in that moment, she did not possess the strength to push him away.

His lips crashed into hers unleashing all the pent-up tension within her over the past days and weeks. She curled her arms around his neck and gave over to her body's craving. She did exactly what she wanted to do and took everything he offered. His hands were in her hair, then on her back pulling her closer so that her breasts were tight to his chest. She could feel his heart beating through his chest. The hard thumping made her nipples tight and hard.

"I have one more question for you," he said breaking the kiss and holding her head, staring deep into her eyes.

Agnes nodded. Words were not forthcoming.

"Will you be my wife?"

The shock of the words made her breath catch in her throat. His wife? Marriage to him? The most eligible man in Scotland and the one who had just kissed her like she was the last woman in the world?

"William, are you certain?"

"Aye, Agnes. I have never been more certain of anything in my life."

"Then the only answer I can give you is, aye, William. I will marry you."

With that he pulled her into his arms and kissed her so profoundly she was sure her grandchildren would feel it. Moments later he pulled away saying something about an early rise and she must be rested. Before she could recall her clan's motto, *Commit thy work to God*, she was in her chamber alone and staring at the closed door.

Had that really just happened?

WILLIAM PACED AS he waited for his instructions to be carried out. He'd written several letters to be dispatched immediately in several directions including Stirling Castle, Mugdock Castle, and Girnigoe. The last had been the hardest. To ask for what he needed without giving the impression his daughter still held her virtue proved difficult and delicate. In the end he was satisfied with his letter and couldn't wait to see what the results would be once they arrived.

Over the next several days, William stole kisses from Agnes whenever he could, but was careful not to let himself become too aroused as to risk their passion ruining their wedding night. It was to be perfect; he had left not one detail out in his letter to her father.

They'd made haste through Grant, Ross, and Munroe lands for obvious reasons, but the haste worked well in his favor as he would that much sooner claim her as his bride and spend his life pleasing her.

Now just a couple miles from her home, he was nervous for the first time in quite a long time. Not even when he had to address the clan for the first time or met the king and accepted his title could compare to this moment.

Soon they were trotting down the long pathway toward the tall tower with the sea in full view beyond. He could understand her belief in mythology having now seen this view firsthand. The castle was not overly large, but sat atop a cliff that seemed to hang out over the sea.

They passed over a bridge and through a stone archway to enter the inner courtyard. The outer visage was deceiving, for what lay inside was much larger than he had anticipated. Properly stocked, this castle would be safe haven for months if needed.

He dismounted first then helped Agnes to the ground. Before he could form another thought, a deep voice sounded behind him.

Agnes darted around him to leap into her father's arms. He was a big man, almost as tall as he, but thicker around the middle and had a burly look about him. His hair was bright red, and he wore a thick beard, but the eyes were unmistakable. Icy blue, like his daughter.

"Father, I have so much to tell you."

"Aye, daughter, I already know far more than you think."

She leaned back from him and then looked at William. He

wanted to keep some surprises to himself and so shrugged and said, "I know nothing of what your father speaks."

He then came forward and grasped the man's arm in greeting.

"Montrose, it has been far too long, and I am pleased to see you are well."

"Aye, my lord. I thank you for your hospitality."

"I haven't given it yet," he said with a twinkle in his eyes. He was going to make William squirm, and rightly so. He'd have done exactly the same if a similar circumstance had befallen his sister.

"Father!" Agnes said and swatted his arm.

"I have one question for you both first."

William knew what the question was though Agnes didn't appear so. Her cheeks were not yet flushed but they would be.

"Is my daughter intact?" His question was fair and plain and said without malice. He was a father doing his duty and expecting the respect that demanded.

"Aye, my lord. Your daughter has not been sullied or harmed in any way. Her virtue is perfectly intact."

"So why the long list of requests including her hand?"

"Your daughter is a beautiful, eligible woman."

"Aye, that she is."

"And I am a suitable match."

"That you are. And—"

He was going to make him say it before he'd even said it to her.

"And as my long list of requests should prove, I care for your daughter and want to spend the rest of my life making her happy."

By now, Agnes's cheeks were full-on flushed.

Her father nodded and stroked his beard then narrowed his eyes. After what seemed like an age, he said, "Very well, Montrose. Welcome to the family."

What followed was a bear crushing hug that would have

damaged a weaker man, but William was grateful for the man's acceptance and blessing.

"Thank you for the honor of allowing me to wed your daughter, my lord."

"Ye don't have that yet," a strong female voice said from behind the earl. "Not until I lay eyes on ye and determine for myself if you're worthy of our Agnes."

She was a small woman who packed a large personality into her tiny frame. He could only imagine the dynamic between the two of them if they ever disagreed.

"Now bend down and let me see you proper," she said. She took his face in her tiny hands and looked into his eyes with no fear. "If you ever do anything to cause grief to my Agnes, I'll box your ears, and I don't care how tall the ladder has to be for me to climb up and do it."

"I understand, my lady, and I promise."

"All that remains then is for you to ask her with us as witness."

They'd already done that, but he'd do it a thousand times over if it meant being one step closer to making her his.

William turned to Agnes who stood there wide-eyed and wringing her hands.

He took her hands in his and said, "Agnes Sinclair, daughter of the Chief of Clan Sinclair and the Earl of Caithness, will you be my wife and make me the happiest man in all of Scotland?"

"Aye, William, I will." She smiled as he kissed the back of both hands and took hers in his as they turned to address her parents.

"I have only one thing to debate, Montrose."

William didn't think he'd forgotten anything. "Of course, my lord."

"Well then, two things. *I* am the happiest man in all of Scotland and that is not up for debate." He kissed the top of his wife's head. "And now we are family, you will call me Hugh."

"I concur then on both counts."

Agnes's mother then whisked her away to somewhere inside the castle leaving William and Hugh alone. There was much more to be said, and it could not be done with the ladies present.

"Will you take some ale with me in my solar?"

"Aye, I would like that. There is much I could not include in my letter."

"You managed to include quite a lot," he said with a grin and slapped William on the shoulder.

He liked Hugh immediately. There would be no back doors with this man who would be forthcoming about his knowledge of his brother and of the others mentioned in the missives.

Once seated in the man's solar, William took the time to look around. The window overlooking the sea was covered with glass panes with thin metal bars running diagonally to one another. He marveled at how pristine they were considering the constant onslaught of sea spray.

"We hang men from the roof to clean them," Hugh said not cracking a smile.

William couldn't tell if he was serious or if it was a small way of keeping him on guard from a protective father.

Hugh passed him a rather large tankard filled to the top with ale.

"Now that is the best ale you will ever have."

William took a sip and though it was heavy and strong, it was surprisingly smooth.

"Aye, I believe it might be."

Hugh winked. "An ancient recipe from the monks of Iona themselves. Or so I'm told." His head fell back and boisterous laughter erupted from within him.

"Now," he said after he'd settled. "Tell me all about what my conniving brother has done this time."

William recapped the entirety of the plot. To his credit, Hugh did not interrupt or offer any expression or noise to indicate whether he believed any or all of it. So William left out no detail including what the king had indicated about Agnes, what his intentions had been, and that the queen felt her innocent.

"And what do you believe, Montrose?"

"Obviously I believe she had no part in it and was not supportive of your brother's planning. Though I do understand from her, he tried to school her on the journey to Stirling."

"School her how?"

"He told her of certain clan histories and made her repeat and memorize their war cry."

"Loyalty is everything," Hugh said.

He would have been aware of the clans or portion of clans who opposed the current king, but how much did he know of the combined group of men who went so far as to plan an attack or even an assassination on the king and his queen? William believed Hugh to be on the right side of the situation, but how far would he go to protect his fellow Highlanders? That question would remain unanswered.

CHAPTER NINE

H ER MOTHER LED her straight to her chamber with no stopping along the way. Agnes found that peculiar considering she'd been aware of her coming and would have thought there would be a meal prepared in their hall.

"I want you to show me all your lovely gowns and tell me all about this earl of yours."

"How did you know the queen ordered gowns for me?"

"Your earl included it in his letter to your father."

"And what else did this letter contain?"

She was curious now. Her mother was behaving in an odd manner, and she had a sneaking suspicion they were up to something.

"I don't know of anything else," she said. "Your father only told me about the gowns."

"You have never been good at telling falsehoods, mother. What else was in the letter?"

Placing her hands on her hips, she said, "I will not reveal what I know as I have been asked not to. And I will obey."

"Who asked you not to say?"

"The earl. He has made some requests and asked us to remain quiet until such time as he can reveal it all to you when he is ready. Do not press me further, Agnes."

Her mother's lips were pressed into a hard line as though it was a struggle to hold in the words she wanted to blurt. She would concede, for William's sake. For if he had put so much effort into a surprise for her, she would honor it.

"Very well, that chest there is one from the queen," she said pointing to a chest that had been placed at the foot of her bed.

Her chamber seemed so much smaller now since she'd stayed at Stirling Castle. This one held all her childish fantasies of endless balls and fancy masques. Her reality was far more of an adventure than she had ever imagined. In the end she returned betrothed to a man she—what? Loved? She wasn't so sure of that, but she did care for him enough that she could be happy with him.

The whole business had happened so fast she wasn't sure what love even was. In spite of that down to her toes, she had no hesitation in marrying him.

"Och, this one is lovely, Agnes," her mother said as she pulled out the deep blue gown she'd worn on the night she met William.

"I have worn that one already which is why 'tis on top of the others. They are all just as beautiful as this one."

Her mother rummaged through the chest until she pulled out a crimson brocade gown similar in style to the blue.

"Och, this will do quite nicely," she said quietly.

"Will do for what?"

Her mother jumped as if she'd forgotten Agnes was in her company.

"What? Oh nothing. I was just thinking out loud."

Her mother placed the gown on her bed and smoothed out the layers. A knock at the door revealed her father's steward and some of the other manservants carrying their wooden tub and many buckets of steaming water.

"Place it there," her mother said, pointing to a spot near the fire.

Once the tub was filled and the men gone, her mother helped her out of her gown and into the tub. She fussed around with various aromatic additions like lavender, some kind of scented milk that made her skin feel smooth, and dried rosehips. Her mother didn't often assist her in a bath, but at those times they would talk about all sorts of things. Agnes was close to both her parents in so many different ways.

"Where did you get all this?"

"Never you mind, child. A mother is allowed to have her own secrets you know."

She didn't want to envision her mother having a luxurious bath, but she supposed the woman was entitled to it.

"You haven't told me about your earl. Beside the fact that you brought home a man with a title, which was never critical, I don't really know anything about how you feel about him or how he came to be the one to return you to us."

Agnes hadn't thought much on it until now. Fin had brought her straight to William when they'd entered the hall. Until now, she thought he was there by coincidence. Interesting.

"I met him before I met the king and queen," she said. "Their chamberlain escorted me to the feast in the hall and he was just there."

The more she thought of it, the stranger it was. He'd spoken to Fin about introducing her. Had he anticipated her arrival and if so, why?

"Well, he is a fine-looking man, I will give you that."

Agnes smiled. He was almost too handsome and seemingly unaware of the many heads that turned when he passed through a crowd.

"But looks aren't everything. Your father was quite a looker in his younger days, and still is in my eyes."

"You and father have a special bond."

"Aye, that we do, but we work at it, Agnes. We don't always agree on everything."

She was well aware of that aspect of her parents' relationship. She'd seen them fall into a horrible row one moment and then her father would pick her mother up and they would disappear into their chamber for hours.

"Agnes, how well do you know him?"

"I know him well enough, as well as anyone knows their betrothed before the wedding."

"You are not obligated to marry him if you do not wish," she said as she brushed Agnes's wet hair.

Agnes leaned back and let the warm water and aromas relax her body.

"I feel no obligation, mother. You do not need to worry about that."

"And what do you feel?"

"I feel like my tongue freezes whenever he is near. My belly feels like it will fly apart at any moment and my face runs hot." She had no intention of sharing some more intimate sensations with her mother of all people.

"That, my love, is called attraction, and no money or title can buy it. From that passion and love can grow, and that is all I needed to know."

Agnes turned to her mother who had tears forming in her eyes. She wrapped her arms around Agnes and said, "My sweet wee lassie, I am so happy for you. He is a good man by your father's estimation, and I know you will be happy together."

"Thank you, Mother."

"Now, let's get you out of the tub before you catch your death and get you ready for your surprise—I mean ready for the meal we have planned."

"All is well, Mother. I don't want to spoil whatever it is either."

As her hair dried, she enjoyed watching her mother root through a large satchel. She pulled out one of the silk shifts, brushed the fabric between her thumb and forefinger, and grinned. "You'll wear this on your wedding night," she said and stuffed it back into the satchel. "No need to tempt either of you until vows are exchanged."

Agnes's cheeks burned at the comment, so she kept her head turned to not draw any attention. She did not want to have any conversation about how the fabric aroused her and of the fantasies they evoked.

Her mother pulled out one of Agnes's finer linen shifts from her old wardrobe and placed it on the bed. Several tugs and ties later, she was fully dressed and ready to discover what William had planned.

Her mother left to change and insisted Agnes wait for her father to escort her below stairs. Thankfully, the wait was not overly long. She'd been standing near the window looking out over the sea when he knocked then entered her chamber. She turned to him and noted his formal dress. She'd rarely seen her father in anything other than his leine and plaid, but today on top of his leine, he wore a tanned leather tunic with their clan sash across his chest and woolen trews with long boots. His sword was fastened at his waist, and his hair was tied back.

"Father, you look wonderful," she said.

He wore a huge smile as he came toward her with his arms outstretched.

"Ahh, my wee sweet lass. You are the most beautiful creature I ever beheld, and I am so very proud of you."

"Shall we collect Mother and head downstairs?"

"Your mother is already below and waiting for us."

Her curiosity was on bust. The most logical thought was that he had them prepare a betrothal celebration and perhaps invited some guests from the village. She would know soon enough!

Agnes and her father reached the bottom of the stairs and crossed the inner courtyard toward the hall.

When the doors opened and she stepped inside, she could not believe her eyes. They'd decorated the hall top to bottom in garland and whatever flowers they could find. Tables were adorned with vases full of them and trenchers were laid out for guests. Servants were all in a row and smiling at her.

Her gaze trailed the length of the hall until her breath caught. At the head was William and standing next to him was Father Alasdair.

This was no betrothal celebration. This was her wedding!

WILLIAM'S HEART THUDDED in his chest like a wild buck during rutting season. He knew the moment her eyes grew wide and realization dawned on her what was going on and he prayed she would not oppose.

She and her father advanced toward him and he couldn't tear his eyes away from her. The dark-crimson gown somehow accentuated her mesmerizing eyes even more than the blue he loved so much, if that was even possible. Cut straight across her breasts, he could make out their fullness beneath the gown and shifted knowing that in a few short hours, he would need to fantasize no longer.

The next moments were a blur as they exchanged vows and the priest said the words he'd been dying to hear.

"You may kiss your bride."

William wasted no time. He took her face in his hands and kissed her lightly, well aware of her father standing to her side.

"Do you like your surprise?"

Her smile lifted his heart to soaring.

"Aye, my lord, I do love this surprise."

"No more of that," he said trying to sound stern. "You will now refer to me as husband or by my given name, wife."

Her cheeks grew that lovely shade of pink to which he was favorably accustomed by now. He took her hand and turned them toward the folks who had been available to attend on such short notice. Many from the close-by village of Wick together with her family and some of the household staff made for a modest gathering, but he was pleased to have that many come to witness their nuptials and bear witness to the joining of their houses.

"Dear gentlefolk, I thank you for joining us in this celebration this day," William said. He'd previously been granted permission from her father to introduce his new wife. "I would like to introduce my wife, Lady Graham, the Countess of Montrose."

He was pleased when the guests curtseyed or bowed. He intended to ensure the evening was perfect in every way.

Her parents both hugged her and they all made their way to the tables. When she sat on her chair and spied the decorations before her, she tilted her head back, laughter erupting from her. The sound thrilled him.

Her father had confessed his delight in the request to have someone whittle tiny carvings of the monster from Loch Ness as well as one of Bregdi.

"This is my wedding gift to you, wife," he said. "Now you may lock them into battle any time you like and determine for yourself which would be the victor."

"This is the best gift I've ever received," she said through a watery smile and squeezed her hand. "How did you manage all this while we traveled?"

"I told you, I sent word to your father, and he complied with every wish."

"Aye, and some of it was not easy. The best—"

"Will turn out perfectly," William cut him off.

"Aye, aye, I shall say no more."

"Well, whatever it is, surely cannot top all this."

He leaned in close to her so that only she could hear. "You haven't gotten your best gift yet."

Her breath caught and she looked around him. He knew no one would say anything about him privately addressing her. And he couldn't wait to undress her. Politeness dictated they remain for the entirety of the meal, and her father had asked they stay for the first of the entertainment.

Throughout the meal he caught her gaze and marveled at her beauty. He caught her a couple times smiling at her sea monster toys and grinning.

"You like your gifts."

She glanced up and caught his eye. "Aye, that I do, husband."

"And how do you plan to thank me?"

"I am certain I will think of some way that will please you." Her words were barely above a whisper.

Her father scraped his chair back and stood. "I am sure I speak for everyone here when I say we are happy for you to take your leave," he said as he winked at William. "We will not keep you any longer when you are scarce aware we exist. I bid you both good eve!"

William needed no further encouragement. He was on his feet in an instant and pulling back Agnes's chair. She looked positively mortified. She wouldn't be for long.

Graciously accepting all the well wishes, he led her out of the hall and through the joviality inside, across the inner courtyard to the staircase leading to the chambers.

"Which one is the green room?" he asked as they topped the stairs.

"Down at the end of the hall on the right," she said. "Did Father say that was to be our chamber for the evening?"

"He said it is appropriate for a husband and wife as it is away from the other chambers."

When they were almost to the door, he picked her up and once inside kicked the door closed with his boot.

Now they were finally alone he turned her to him. "Are you truly accepting of this? Of me?"

"Aye, William. I confess it is all happening so fast, but I feel in my entire being this is the correct path and you and I are meant to be together."

Her words were a relief. He tilted her chin up and stared hard into her eyes. He saw neither hesitation nor fear, but the same passion he'd seen every time he kissed her.

William removed his belt and tunic and reached for her. He took his time with his first kiss with his new wife. This was a time for her to be cherished. He brushed his lips across hers and loved it when she pressed her body into his. He was already aroused just by the sight of her, but if she rubbed against him, he'd not last near as long as he wanted.

He pulled back enough to stroke his fingers along her neck to the top of her breasts. Her breathing became ragged as he untied her bodice and pulled it from her body. She was already fiddling with the skirt ties, so he pushed her hands away.

"I want to do that," he said and brushed his lips across the tender flesh below her ear. "You are mine to enjoy, and I promise you pleasure like you have never known."

She grasped his arms as if to steady herself and groaned low in her throat when he grazed her neck with his teeth. Her sound made his cock throb.

Once her skirts were untied, he pushed them down and then lifted her out of them with one arm. On the bed he noticed something shiny.

"What's this?" he asked lifting the delicate fabric.

"It would appear my mother is a trickster," she said. "Turn around. I want to wear this for you."

He would indulge her in this as it seemed important to her. He turned his back and removed his shirt and boots and untied his trews. He would leave them on as long as he could stand. After what seemed like an age she said, "Turn around."

William had seen beautiful women in scarce clothing, but this was like nothing with which he was familiar. Her nipples were rock hard, and her round breasts and full hips were perfectly accentuated by this pale shiny fabric that shimmered when she walked toward him.

Agnes encircled his neck with her arms and pressed her body to his. The sensation of her breasts and the fabric on his chest tightened his loins to near madness. It was time to inflict some torture of his own. William picked her up and placed her on the bed then crawled up beside her. He slid his hand up her leg until he reached her hip then reached around to cup her bottom and pull her closer. She would feel him now, the full length of him.

"I ache to be inside you," he said as his mouth closed over hers.

William slid his hand inside her shift and upward until he reached her slick heat. Her body bucked when he pressed one finger inside, then two. She was hot and ready for him, but he would make this sweet torture last as long as he could.

Through the fabric he tugged at her nipple with his teeth ever so gently in time with the rhythmic stroking below. Faster and faster he stroked and watched as her body tensed and pulsed around his fingers. She gasped and bucked and called out his name, holding onto his arm as to will him to push deeper and harder.

When her climax ended, he stripped off her shift and began again. He would see to her utter and complete satisfaction before he took his own.

CHAPTER TEN

S HE'D DIED AND entered the eternal plane. There was nothing more to it. The things he made her feel were surely not for this realm. William had taken her to a height she never knew existed until that moment. She now understood how much tension she'd been under really since the moment they met. Her body had known what it wanted all along.

William's broad chest covered her, and he'd shifted his hips so that he was wedged between her legs, though he still wore his trews. But she could feel every inch of his hard member and longed to know what it would feel like when he did enter her.

He kissed her mouth with such passion she could scarcely draw breath and though she'd just been pleasured, his mouth and hands and body on her quickly set her pulse racing again. When he pinched her nipple, hot desire shot to her core. She could feel wet heat between her legs, and she couldn't resist raising her hips to his in invitation.

"Not yet, my wanton wife," he whispered. "I have more to show you first."

William rolled to his side and took one nipple into his mouth sucking hard. At the same time, he drove two fingers inside her again making stars form behind her eyes. He alternated between nipping and thrusting and just as she was about to climax, he stopped.

She opened her eyes long enough to see him kick off his trews and a heartbeat later he was between her legs with the tip of his hard member pressing into her. He hovered above her and she looked down to see the size of him.

"Put your legs around my waist," he said as he pushed in ever so slightly.

The pressure was great, but her desire tempered the discomfort. William scooped his arms under her shoulders and held her head in his hands. He kissed her softly as he entered her a little bit at a time and then pulled out only to enter a little more each time.

She was grateful he'd been gentle and by the time he had fully entered her, her desire raged again. She moved her hips in time with his and increased her tempo when he wasn't moving as fast as she would like.

"William, please," she said as he was still agonizingly slow.

"I do not wish to hurt you," he said.

"I am not hurt," she said and placed her hand on his cheek. "I want you to love me the way you want to."

He smiled and kissed her hard as he thrust deep within her. She couldn't help the groan that escaped her lips or the way she clung to his shoulders, and he thrust into her faster and harder with each passing moment.

The moment was upon her again and she felt the sensation low in her spine which spread throughout her whole body. William tensed above her then shook for a few moments for what seemed like an age as he hovered over her, still inside, his breath ragged.

He lay by her side and pulled her close to him. Her heart still pounded hard and her breathing ragged for long moments after their release.

She had no words. For what could be said of what they had experienced? Was it like that for everyone, or did they possess something rare and timeless? Would it always be that way between them or was it just because it was her first time?

"Tell me what you are thinking," he said.

"I am thinking what we have shared is some kind of magical spell."

"It is of a sort," he said.

"Does that mean not everyone finds this?"

"It means that most people have a version of this, but not to this degree, no. This is special. You are special," he said and kissed the top of her head.

She shivered as the night air cascaded in through the open window. They pulled back the covers and crawled beneath them, curling into one another. She loved the way their bodies melded one into the other and how his arms felt wrapped around her. She drifted, feeling more satisfied and more safe than she ever had in her life.

Waking sometime later she realized he was not wrapped around her anymore, rather with his head between her legs and his tongue doing all sorts of wickedly delicious things. The arousal she thought she'd been dreaming of hit her hard in her awakened state and she climaxed within seconds of waking.

She was still pulsing as he pressed into her with his rigid member. This was not the slow start from earlier; he rammed into her, driving her higher and higher and to her shock, she climaxed again as he stiffened above her. She'd not thought that was at all possible.

"By God, you will be the death of me," he said as he lay by her side.

"Shouldn't that be the other way around?" she asked and slapped his buttocks. She didn't know what possessed her, but she couldn't resist anything about him.

"Give me ten minutes, woman, and then you can have more," he said through a sleepy yawn. Moments later he was snoring.

She turned on her side to snuggle into his side as he lay flat on his back. In his sleep he put his arm around her and pulled her in tight to him. How long she lay there wide awake and staring at the lines on his face in the moonlight she didn't know.

Her fingers traced the straight bridge of his nose and then his full lips. He was such a treasure she wanted to memorize him in any way she could, for surely this was too good to last forever. People didn't get to have this and keep it too. Otherwise, they would never leave their chambers.

Twice more he woke her like that during the night, and she was certain she would not walk the next day, but she didn't care. Her soreness was worth the connection their passion forged. For she'd never been so connected to another human being in her life, and she was not sure it was even possible any other way.

Now she understood what love was. And she was well on her way to loving him. She doubted she could function in a world where there was no William.

How silly her fantasies had been as a maid and before going to Stirling. She hadn't even known what she'd been wishing for and thanked all the forces that had brought the two of them together.

"Are you not worn out yet?" he asked.

It was only then she realized he was awake and staring at her. He brushed some of her hair from her forehead and kissed the cleared spot.

"I don't want this to end."

"What makes you think it will end? We are married and will have our whole lives together."

"Aye, you say that, but what if something happens to you? I could not bear it."

"Shh, love. Nothing is going to happen to either one of us. We have many years ahead of us to torment one another as your parents do."

"Do you promise?"

"Aye, I promise. Nothing will happen to me or you. Now close your eyes. We have to break our fast with your parents in just a couple of hours, and my wanton wife kept me up all night begging me to pleasure her again and again. Truly, woman, you are most demanding."

She did as he asked and closed her eyes, but sleep would not come quickly. She had a foreboding sense that in the balance of the world, something this good would come at a price. That was the way of things and who were they to test fate?

Agnes curled into him once more and slid her hands across his thick chest then closed her eyes. His irresistible scent of clean air and leather drew her toward slumber and at some point she did manage to sleep.

HER WORDS HAUNTED him as they dressed to meet her parents. He threw on a fresh pair of trews and leine and fastened his regular tunic and belt before donning his boots and moving to the bed to see how she fared.

He understood the fear, for he too had never experienced what they had shared but they could not treat it as though it were a fleeting gift. They'd found one another against all the odds in the world, and he planned to spend his life being grateful and living for the here and now.

Her hand reached over to his side of the bed, and she sat up after swiping it back and forth and finding it empty.

She blinked at him a couple of times then grinned through her sleepy expression. "I thought you had left."

"Never," he said. "I was just about to go see about arranging a bath for you."

"That sounds glorious," she said and leaned back to stretch, her breasts jutting upward. How was it possible that the sight stirred his loins after the night of lovemaking they'd had?

"If you keep doing that, I will not be leaving this chamber for the day, and you will need more than a bath to soothe you."

She laughed and pulled the sheets up to cover herself. "Very well, go see to a bath, and can you see if there's any food about.

I'm ravenous."

"We are to break our fast with your parents this morn."

"Aye, but Cook always leaves a platter out for early risers. His name is Connor and he will be in the kitchen already. Tell him I asked and he will look after you."

"Is this the same cook you stole sweet treats from all those years ago?"

"Aye, the very one!"

William kissed her again and left the chamber. He was pleased to see a tub waiting outside the chamber and quickly lifted it inside then went in search of hot water. He could kill two birds with one stone if he found the cook and a couple servants in the same place.

He was not disappointed. The din in the kitchen could be heard well outside of the structure, which was joined with all the others, but like the hall, could only be accessed from outside.

"I am told to come find Connor," William said as he entered the kitchen.

A round aging man with a kind face shot forward. "I told ye. I said our wee one would want a plate come the morn. Welcome in, m'lord. We will see ye tended to. Is it a bath ye be needing? Ale?"

The man seemed like he couldn't do enough for him.

"It is a pleasure to meet you, Connor. Is it possible to get some hot water for the lady's bath? And aye, she requested a plate."

"The water is already hot," he said. "I saw to that first as I thought she would like that too."

"You know your lady well," William said in a kind tone. He liked households where the serving staff genuinely cared for the family. It meant they had been treated well, and that said a great deal about the earl and his clan.

"I have known the lass her whole life," he said. "Loved her even when she stole buns from the kitchen."

"She thinks you didn't know it was her."

"And I intend to keep it that way if ye please, m'lord. I have spent many delightful moments remembering her giggles as she ran off, treat in hand."

William placed his hand over his heart. "She will never hear it from my lips."

"I thank ye, m'lord. Now, I will have all of this sent up to yer chamber immediately. Is there aught else I can offer ye, m'lord?"

William shook his head. "No, thank you, Connor. You are a gem in this household, to be sure."

William loved the way the man's chest puffed from the praise. He left him and the kitchen to go in search of her father whom he presumed would be up and about as well.

Finding him in the hall, he approached and spied that he too preferred an early plate. He stopped eating and wiped his mouth when William entered.

"You caught me," he said with a small laugh.

"Not at all, Hugh, keep eating."

"Thank you," he said. "By the time the ladies are ready for the real morning meal, my stomach would have eaten itself. I trust my daughter is well this morn?"

"Aye, that she is and I have just come from the kitchen where water has been warmed for her bath and a platter of food readied to send up. I will leave her to some peace and check on her in a while."

"Then you can join me and share some of this with me. No need for you to wait either."

"How fared the entertainment after?"

"It was a wonderful time, but we saved your surprise for this evening as I am sure you would wish."

"Does your wife know about it?"

"No, I could barely keep her from telling everyone about the whittled figures. I knew Agnes always enjoyed those stories, but I didn't know quite how much until you mentioned it."

"You should have seen her off in her own fantasies practically telling these tales by expression alone. I knew it was a special part of her growing up here so close to the sea."

"Aye, 'tis fairly remote. Her mother and I had little interest in court. We are happy securing the king's interest here in the north as there are many who would oppose him, as you now know."

"That I do. You are sure none of the men listed in the missives are close at hand and can get to her?"

"I am as certain as I can be," Hugh said. "I have sent scouts and I have spies in particular towns to watch the comings and goings."

"I am pleased to hear it. I too have sent direction for the same."

"How long do you intend to stay?"

"I will speak with my wife about that today. I appreciate the security of this castle, but I know how to defend my own."

"I can appreciate that. This castle is impenetrable. And we are stocked here so we could sustain a siege for a year if need be."

"All respect intended, Hugh. I do not intend to be anywhere under siege for a year. This business will be taken care of and soon. The king and those loyal to him will see to it."

Hugh put his hands up. "Ye'll get no argument from me. But I'm here to tell you these rebels are ferocious in their belief that the king is false and that he should be eliminated together with his English wife."

William didn't doubt that for a second, but a handful of men was no match for the king's guard and the forces his allies could raise to defend him. And he would protect his family with his own life if need be.

He thought back to Agnes's words from earlier. Did she have some sense of what was to come? He would keep her safe. It was a vow he'd made to her, to himself, and now to her father.

"You do not ever have to worry about the security of your daughter when we leave this place," he said. "I will never let anything happen to her."

"I am glad to hear that, William. Now eat some food and let us lighten the mood for the day. I would like to take you on a tour of these lands this afternoon. Perhaps then you will have a better understanding of the degree to which the natural landscape protects us here at Grinigoe. And what the landscape does not protect, the sea does."

He was coming to know these people to have a deep belief in myth and legend. In the far reaches of the north coast and relatively isolated, he supposed it was natural for stories to emerge fueled from the unknown and an environment that could be harsh. It was believable that folks could cling to superstition; if I toss the salt to the left, I won't be whisked away at night by some unseen force.

The story he'd made up for Agnes and her reaction to it was proof that this was an important part of her heritage, and he couldn't wait to see her reaction when she received the biggest surprise he had devised for her.

William finished his meal and thanked Hugh for his hospitality and advice. The man was to be respected and trusted, so he would heed his words well in addition to knowing his own mind. They would weather this threat.

The biggest issue for him was how to keep Agnes from understanding the full extent of it. He would not have her living in constant fear or looking over her shoulder. Nay, he would keep her entertained and ensure she enjoyed every moment of their wedding festivities.

When he returned to their chamber, he found her bathed and brushing her long hair by the fire. The platter was empty save for a few crumbs and she wore only her shift. She beamed at him when he entered and his heart squeezed tight. She was his prize. His gift for living in this world and nothing would take that from him.

CHAPTER ELEVEN

L OST IN HER own thoughts, when the door to her chamber closed, she jumped. Turning quickly, she was relieved to find William coming toward her with a warm smile on his beautiful face.

"I did not mean to startle you, wife," he said in a quiet tone.

"I was merely lost in my thoughts," she said. She hoped he wouldn't pry, because she didn't want to seem like a constant worrier, but she couldn't shake her dark thoughts, and that had never happened to her before.

"Well then let us put different thoughts in that beautiful head of yours."

William took the brush from her hand and lifted her hair so he could brush it. She watched as he drew it to his face and inhaled.

"You smell like a fresh meadow," he whispered. "I will never tire of this."

His words warmed her heart. She was convinced what they had was rare and beautiful, which was what made it all the more precious to protect.

"And I shall never tire of the way you look at me."

William cupped her face in his hands and kissed her lips with the lightest touch. Even that light joining was enough for her to want him again. The bath had done its job quite well. Where her body had been stiff and sore from their passionate night, she was now relaxed and limber once again.

Once her hair had dried, she put it into a loose braid and donned a mesh cap. She chose one of her own woolen gowns for the day and would spend some time later finding an appropriate one for the evening. The queen's gifts seemed a wee bit overdone for here, but she was grateful for them just the same.

As she smoothed her skirts into place, she noticed William had become quiet as he stared out her window at the sea.

"'Tis a beautiful view, is it not?"

"Aye, I can see how it would stir the imagination."

She liked that he could appreciate her home and all that which made her who she was. Now more than ever she was curious about his home. The story he'd told her, while false, must have stemmed from somewhere.

"Come," he said before she could ask him anything, "we must go to the hall. Your father has promised me a tour of his lands today and I am quite interested to learn more about this area."

She took his hand and they left the chamber to make their way to the great hall. It remained as it was the evening before with beautiful flowers everywhere, and what had been an evening feast prior was now set for the morning meal. Platters of breads and pastries and Connor's famous buns were laid out on a side table so guests could choose their own preference. She took three buns and some cheese, bread, and poured a goblet of warm mead.

Once they were all seated her mother asked, "How does my daughter fare this morn?"

"I am well, mother," Agnes said.

"I am pleased to hear that," her father said chiming in. "There'd be hell to pay if it were otherwise." He then raised his goblet to William who took the words in stride.

The meal continued on with some small talk about the night before and the one to come. Agnes understood that their presence was to be expected, but she was fast forming the opinion that she did not want to share her new husband, rather keep him all to herself. For her parents' sake, however, she would go along with their wishes and partake in the festivities as long as they wanted. The norm was three days, so that was hopefully what they had in mind. This evening would be the biggest of the feasts as it was custom the bride and groom did not stay late on their wedding night. But the night after was something different, and William had mentioned a surprise for her as if the toy creatures were not enough.

God had been kind to her. Despite the circumstances that had brought them together, it was in her mind a perfect match. In all ways.

Once the meal was over, her father announced he would take William away for the remainder of the day. "Kiss your wife," he said and William didn't hesitate.

One swift kiss later and he was gone.

She turned to her mother. "Well, what are we doing today?"

"We," she said reaching for Agnes's hands, "are going to do what proper ladies do, which is be doted on and gossip. I want to hear all about the ladies at court and how you plan to conduct yourself now you are a countess."

While the title was not unfamiliar to her, she had not really given much thought to what that actually meant. She'd always been treated with the proper respect at home, but theirs was a far less formal existence than what she'd seen at court. Save for Fin, all servants were firmly in their place with the divide clearly visible.

And that was one more thing she wondered about with William's home. There was no indication he was a firm laird, but folks were known to put on airs in company and behave far different at home.

She and her mother passed the afternoon with their needlepoint near the hearth in the hall chatting about things of little importance. Agnes time and again looked toward the door when she heard a noise, hoping the men had returned. She would have liked to go with them, but after her night with William, she would not want to be on horseback all day. The thought made her smile and squirm a little.

"Are you unwell?" her mother asked.

"I am well, mother. Why do you ask?"

"Because you have hardly said a word while I have prattled on all day and you keep looking at the door. Now you are smiling to yourself. Am I even here?"

Her mother was not really mad, rather teasing her and skirting around the questions she obviously really wanted to ask.

Agnes placed her needlework in her lap and her hands on top. "Is there anything you are particularly curious about?"

Her mother shook her head. "Nay, lass. I merely want to be sure you are well. That you—that he was gentle."

The color of her cheeks must have turned bright crimson for the heat that now burned them. She could not talk to her mother about the rambunctious lovemaking she and her new husband shared the night before. But she was curious about a thing or two.

"Is it normal to—"

Her sentence trailed off as she tried to find the words.

"To what?"

"To like it?"

"Like what? The act?"

She wanted to bury her head beneath the rocks on the shoreline.

"Aye," she said in a quiet voice. "And to want to do it a lot?"

Through her own pink cheeks, her mother said, "Nay, my wee lassie who is wee no more. That is a rare and beautiful thing that our lord only blesses the most fortunate of couples. Your father and I—"

Agnes put her hands up. Nay. She would not hear anything about her parents in that way. She could not bear to have that discussion in addition to the difficulty she had talking about herself.

"Mother, I do not wish to be a disrespectful daughter, but I do not want to hear about my parents' activity. 'Tis hard enough talking about my own."

"Very well, I will not tell you anything other than your father and I are fortunate too."

"Mother!" Agnes said before placing her hands over her ears. She couldn't be sure, but she was fairly certain no child wanted to think of their parents that way.

"It is of no real concern, Agnes. But if it bothers you that much, I will not say another word." She pursed her lips together and with her thumb and forefinger turned an imaginary lock on her lips as if to seal them together forever.

Agnes knew better. Now the topic was broached, her mother would find a way to make her opinions and points known. She always did. God help her.

Not long after, the men returned. Agnes couldn't help but laugh when her father promptly kissed her mother's cheek. When she looked toward Agnes and wagged her brows, Agnes couldn't hold it in any longer. She burst into gales of laughter after which her mother joined.

"What did I miss?" her father asked.

"Nothing you need to worry about," her mother said. "Let's say it's an inside jest."

That last comment sent Agnes into another fit of laughter. William merely stood by and watched. When she finally settled down, he came to her and kissed her cheek.

"I missed you," he whispered.

She wasn't laughing anymore when she saw the heat in his eyes. He took her hand and walked with her out of the hall. The sound of her mother's laughter followed her.

WILLIAM PRACTICALLY DRAGGED her to their chamber. Once the door was closed firmly behind him, he reached for her. Picking her up, he placed her on the bed and lay on top of her. He kissed her hard and fast and pressed his already erect cock onto her through their clothes.

"I need you now," he whispered as he gazed into her eyes looking for a reflection of the passion raging through him.

"Aye, William, quickly."

He stood up by the bed, loving the way her eyes devoured him as he pulled off his tunic and leine then unbuttoned his trews. He reached for her and pulled her to standing. She looked confused as he turned her around and bent her over the bed before him.

"Do you trust me?"

"Aye," she said without hesitation.

He lifted her skirt up to and over her waist revealing her perfect bottom. He smoothed his hands over it and pressed his still covered cock onto her. He then traced his fingers lightly along her inner thighs until he came to her slick heat. She was more than ready for him, and he would show her yet another way he could pleasure her.

William slid two fingers inside her and stroked. When she moaned, he slipped in a third. She orgasmed around his fingers almost immediately and while still pulsing, he shoved his pants down, positioned his cock, and entered her.

Agnes's body shook as he slowly entered her and withdrew only to drive himself deeper within her with each thrust. The sight of him moving in and out of her was almost her undoing. His balls tightened as he gripped her hips and quickened the pace.

Between her groans and pushing back against him for more, he fought his release. He would not let go until he felt her clench around him. Her hands shot out in front of her, and she gripped the coverlet on the bed. She raised herself and pushed back harder against him, panting and groaning.

"Oh, aye! Oh, William!" she whispered with such urgency, he knew her moment was close at hand.

To bring her to an even higher plane he pulled out of her

completely and rubbed the tip of his cock against her then slammed in hard. He repeated this several more times as he watched her head tilt back with her hair sliding to one side.

"Please," she said in a whimper.

He would never deny her. William thrust deep within her, quickening his rhythm until he felt her tighten around him and the familiar and delicious first licks of his own climax hit in the base of his spine. It spread through him like wildfire. His entire body quaked as his release peaked, forming stars behind his eyes. He looked down to see her in much the same state.

William slowed his movements so they could enjoy the last wave of their pleasure. When he was done, he covered her, kicked off his trews, and climbed up on the bed beside her to where she'd crawled.

Her breath was still ragged as he wrapped his arm around her waist pulling her back to his chest and burying his face in her hair.

"I missed you too," she said in a low, laughing voice.

He smiled. "Sleep now, wife," he said. "We have a long night ahead of us."

Moments later, her body relaxed and her breath evened out. He waited until he was sure she was asleep then slipped away from her and pulled an extra quilt up over her.

William sat by the fire and poured himself some ale that had been brought up earlier. It would seem these staff anticipated every desire. He leaned back and let his long legs stretch out before him.

He'd learned much that day from Hugh. Grinigoe was indeed well protected and well situated on Wick Bay. The township of Wick was close enough so that some of the servants could return there after a week's work at the castle. The town was complete with a kirk, blacksmith, tanner, and an inn with a tavern.

He asked about the townsfolk and of the loyalty that could be expected from them. Hugh had been quite forthcoming in mentioning them all, mostly by name, which was encouraging since he was acquainted with each and every family who lived in

Mugdock village.

The one aspect of Sinclair security William was not clear on was the proximity to clans MacKay and Sutherland. Those clans warred with one another frequently, but where Hugh placed himself among those battles, he was not specific. 'Twas fair enough if that man's position was to remain neutral, but if so, why not make that declaration? William feared it was something far more dangerous, even if not malicious. If Hugh was playing both sides, the resulting effect could have far-reaching consequences. Add in the Highland rebels and this was not a place he wanted to remain with his new wife. Of that much he was certain.

Agnes sighed in her sleep drawing his attention to her form. By God he could not have imagined a more perfect match for himself. She was everything and more he could have ever hoped for. That made the dangers around them much more apparent. He needed to get them out of here where there was nowhere to run should they be cornered.

He'd read the names; in addition to the territories they'd crossed to get here, MacKay was included and if that meant the laird, he was not interested in stirring that pot.

For tonight, he would ensure the king's guard was assigned to Agnes and no other. They'd been ever watchful and working in shifts, but they would all have their focus on her until she was safely settled into Mugdock Castle. They would leave the day after next and not one moment later. He would allow the three days of nuptial festivities, but after that they would make the long journey home. There weren't many opportunities to take alternate routes unless he wanted to delay their return significantly, and he most assuredly did not want that.

Agnes stirred on the bed. He loved the way she blinked at him as if she had no idea where she was.

"You still have time to slumber before getting ready if you like," he said.

She sat up and stretched. "My back was cold and I didn't

know where you'd gone."

"I'm just sitting here, wife. Enjoying the quiet before the evening."

She slid off the bed and came to sit in his lap. Curling up, she placed her arms around his neck and put her head on his shoulder.

"Something is troubling you," she said.

"What makes you say that?"

"Because your brows are tight together and your dimples are not showing. They disappear when you frown."

He hadn't realized she had taken such a note of his expressions. This woman of his was far more aware of her surroundings than he'd given credit.

"I was wondering how I'd gotten so fortunate as to have found such a creature as you."

Agnes unlinked her arms and placed her hands on his face.

"William. I want you to promise me one thing and one thing only."

"And what is that?"

"I want you to promise me that you will never lie to me again."

He stared deep into her eyes. She meant it and he wanted to make that promise. But he could not tell her everything. Particularly his suspicions regarding her father's potential involvement with the rebels, even if involuntary. William feared Hugh was turning a blind eye out of a desire to keep the peace. One could still be found guilty of a crime if one was aware of a dangerous plot and did nothing.

"I promise you that I will be as truthful as I can in all things."

"I know you are holding onto information about the Highlanders plotting against the king and queen. I also know you are not being truthful when it comes to my safety. I want you to tell me what has put this level of concern on your face."

"Agnes, it is not that simple."

"It can be," she said. "If you trust me."

"It is not about trusting you. It's about endangering you more. Your father is convinced this castle and its location is the safest place you could be. I disagree and will only rest easy when you are firmly located at Mugdock Castle and our journey is behind us."

"You truly feel I am in danger?"

"Aye, I do now more than ever. Now I have seen the lands surrounding this place and having considered your neighbors, I am convinced it is not safe for you here."

He hated the look of sadness that crept into her eyes. Thankfully she didn't ask any further questions or make any debate with him. He kissed her softly and drew her into an embrace. Nothing on this earth would take her from him.

CHAPTER TWELVE

R UMMAGING THROUGH HER chest of gowns, she rooted until she found the exact one she sought. She might not know the correct number of guards to place on the wall, but she knew every stone in this castle and every hill surrounding it. She was proud of her family and her clan. She would prove to William they were trustworthy and good people.

His words had cut her to her core. How could he think she was not safe in her own home? How could he think her father and their clan were not capable of seeing to her safety?

Agnes smoothed her gown out on the bed. Her mother had it stitched especially for her for the celebration of her eighteenth year. It was finely woven wool of the softest she'd ever worn in a dark green to represent the primary color in their clan flag. With a square neckline and floor-length sleeves, she loved the way it hugged her body. The gown was trimmed with gold embroidery in the shape of rolling waves and even now she wondered how the needlepoint could be so flawless.

She put herself into her gown and waited for one of the maids to come help her with her hair. She would wear none of those hoods like the ladies of court. Nay, she would have hers pinned up with large loose curls, as was expected of a married lady with a head roll matching her gown. She would hold her head high and show him what it is to be a Sinclair, even if she was now a

Graham. She would never compromise who she was.

Once she was fully ready, she waited for William to return to escort her to the hall. As the minutes droned on, her belly tightened. Was she overreacting? She didn't think so. He'd all but insulted her father and their clan, insinuating they were not competent. Agnes paced until a knock finally sounded at the door.

William entered and her breath caught. He was dressed head to toe in black leather. He'd said he wanted to give her time to ready herself and that he would dress in one of the other chambers as he had something he wanted to prepare for the evening's fest.

All the black on his body made his honey eyes all the brighter. His gaze took in the length of her and for long moments they merely stared at one another.

"You are radiant, wife," he said coming toward her.

The sound of his voice drew her back to the present. She lifted her chin, "Aye, husband. I am feeling rather proud at the moment."

He gave her a sideways smile. "You did not like the truths I shared with you earlier."

"I did not. To suggest my father and our clan are incapable of keeping me safe is insulting."

He stopped his advance then and his smile faded. "It was not my intention to offend you, Agnes. I have developed a great deal of respect for your father, your family, and you."

"Yet you feel they are incompetent."

"Nay, I do not. But up here you are cornered with nowhere to go. I do not know your neighbors, but I know of them. I know of the feuds that had claimed many lives. I know of abductions of ladies, and I know of vile plots to slay innocents. But in all of those tales I do not hear the Sinclair name. Why is that?"

"Because we are peaceful," she said. What was he implying?

"Aye, you are peaceful, yet you still hold your own lands. I was pondering on all of this earlier when you asked me to trust you. I have done so and shared my deepest worry with you, and for that you are vexed with me."

"Are you saying my father has an agreement of some sort with both the MacKay and Sutherland?"

"I am saying your circumstance is peculiar. And I am saying I do not feel this is the safest place for you right now considering the very real threat of your uncle's ilk. Agnes," he said and cupped her face, "if anything were to happen to you…" He brushed his lips across hers.

Agnes tried to take in his words. He was worried, anyone could see that. And aye, she'd heard of the extent of the feuds. Some of the stories were downright terrifying.

"Have you spoken of any of this to my father?"

"I have not."

"Then do not. I will show you that you can trust me with your worries. And I will show you that my father is an honorable man."

"I do not doubt that for a moment, Agnes. I truly believe your father to be one of the most honorable men I've ever met. I would not have you believe otherwise. It is my intention to speak to the king on his behalf to secure more permanent protection for him."

"To what end?" she asked. "The castle is secure."

"Aye, a true stronghold. But the townships are exposed and could easily harbor foes."

Agnes had not thought about it like that. She knew most of the villagers, but not all. And it was true, they did not keep a full regiment of guards.

"Will you continue to trust me?" he asked.

"Aye, if you will do the same," she said.

"Excellent," he said. "Now come, we have a wonderful evening to spend together free from worry and clan feuds and plots against the king."

She would do her best to put her concerns aside and enjoy the evening with her clan. She was left in no doubt they would leave here soon. He didn't need to speak the words. It was evident in all the other words he'd said. Was there truth in them? Was she that naive and blind to the ways of the world? She would be more observant, that much she promised herself.

When they entered the hall, it had been transformed again. This time the main table had been pushed to the side. Guests filled small trenchers with food and either stood to mingle with their food or sat at the long table long enough to eat their meal. She liked the informality of the set up.

In front of the hearth were many chairs organized in rows for some future entertainment of which she was not aware. William had promised her a surprise this evening. Was this part of it?

Agnes embraced her mother and walked with her to the food tables. She was surprisingly ravenous considering she'd accomplished little all day. Well, save for the passion she'd shared with her husband. She supposed that was one thing she could trust in.

Once everyone had eaten, her father stood by the hearth, raised his hands, and said, "Welcome all once again to celebrate my sweet wee lassie and her new husband, a man I have lately come to know and for whom I've grown a deep respect. I know my daughter will be in safe hands with him in every way."

Her father's endorsement meant everything to her. If he trusted William's judgment, she would too.

"Come find yourselves a seat and we will begin the evening's entertainment. We invite any and all to take the floor, share a story, sing a tune, or play your pipes. All except Ewen who cannae hold a note to save his life."

Her father tilted his head back and a roar of laughter erupted from him. Poor Ewen loved to sing, but it was more pleasant to listen to the gulls fight each other over the fish guts tossed off the wharf near the town.

One by one, folks presented their talents. Pipes bleated out initial notes until rhythm and melody took over, wee lads tried their hands at singing old tunes, and an elderly lady from Wick told stories of faeries that would steal ye away in the night if ye put yer washing out on the wrong day of the week.

She watched William take it all in and could not help but feel so proud at that moment. These were her people. Her clansmen and women and they were all honorable and good. She would not believe for a minute there was a malicious bone in any of their bodies.

William turned to her and kissed her forehead. "Now it's my turn," he said. "Surprise."

Her jaw opened a little as he stood and made his way to the front of the group. He smiled and winked at her and then raised his hands in the air. Was he about to tell another falsehood? Did he actually have story to tell this time, or was he about to sing? Her full focus and attention was on him as she waited to see what he would do.

WILLIAM TOOK NOTE there were no small children left in the hall, and he was grateful for he didn't want to censor himself.

"My lord Sinclair. I thank you for the honor of this feast and for your hospitality. I have come to house a deep respect for you and your family as well. And especially for my enchanting and spirited new wife, my countess." He placed his hand on his heart and bowed to her.

"This evening, I have planned a special treat for you as I have not done this since I was a young lad. I will tell a story that is so harrowing, and so ghastly, you will not sleep this night, I promise you."

Around the hall, he heard some soft gasps. It was quite a statement to make considering he was aware of the pleasure these people placed on their stories. He'd learned that from Agnes and it was easy to see why.

"This eve I will tell you about Cailleach and how she tried to kill the first kings of Scotland. She is said to be an old woman appearing frail and feeble until you speak to her and then her true nature comes forth."

William walked slowly about the hall rather than staying put in one place. He looked directly at people for emphasis as he began his tale.

"An elder in the village near my castle saw her one night. 'Twas late in the harvest and the nights had gotten close to frost. He'd just shut the horse in the barn for the night and was making his way back to his house when he spied a person up the laneway leaning heavily on a cane.

"'Och, do ye need any help?' he called to her.

"The woman didn't reply, but shuffled toward him slowly. He called to her again and still no reply. When she was almost upon him and he caught the stench of her he gagged. It was as if all the rotting meat for an eon was put into the one place and left to further rot in the hot sun. At that moment, she stood tall and flung away her cape. Her cane grew into a long staff with pointy star shaped ice at the tip. Her skin was full on blue, and her eyes were like the brightest stars in the sky. Her hair was white as snow and hung stringy to the ground and beyond. This was no old lady and no enchantress."

As he spoke, he placed his hand on a man's shoulder from behind him who promptly yelped.

"She touched the ground with the icy part of her staff and frost spread from it. The old man jumped back and tried to escape from its path, but it was too late. When she touched the ground again the frost spread faster. It caught up with him then and moved over his feet, climbed up his legs and chest, his arms, and up to his neck. The only parts of him that were not covered in ice were his heart and his head."

He touched two people's heads also from behind them. Both jumped, then nervously laughed. Those gathered now looked around the hall to follow his movements. Only Agnes kept her gaze forward as if lost in his tale. William made his way to the front of the group and honed in on her.

"She approached him with a sickening smile revealing black teeth. 'You are fortunate you are a good man. For you offered to help me. Otherwise, you would be dead right now.'

"The man was unable to move his limbs or even speak. He stayed there like that while she touched her staff to the ground many more times and in different areas where he could still see her. Many hours passed and as the first streaks of gray crossed the sky, she donned her cloak, the staff returned to a cane, and she once again became a feeble looking old woman. She gave him one last look and disappeared off into the morning mist."

He was now mere inches from her face and practically whispering his tale to her, loving the way she hung on every word.

He stood abruptly, addressing the whole crowd and changing his tone from dark and dramatic to matter of fact.

"How much longer he stood there, he could not say, but it was not until the sun's rays touched him that the frost melted and he was free from her curse. When he managed to stumble into his house, his feet were black from frostbite, and he eventually lost four toes and two fingers. Thankfully his wife was an accomplished healer. But he never forgot the sight of her or her stench. And he was never caught outside at night in late fall ever again."

William stood back as the crowd took in his story. Many were on the edge of their seat, including Agnes, whose eyes were wide and her mouth slightly open. She stood and slowly clapped. Moments later others joined in, and the hall erupted with cheers and men coming to shake his hand.

Pushing past them all was Agnes. She looked up at him with a beaming smile. "Thank you. That was the best gift you've ever given me. You have a natural talent. True, I thought Mother was going to faint dead away."

He kissed the top of her head. He enjoyed the look on all their faces as he drew them into his story, but he particularly loved seeing Agnes so transfixed. He would have to bring in the actual elder from the village to meet her.

"But is it true?" someone asked, whom he couldn't quite see.

"Aye, 'tis true. My wife can meet him and send word of him when we return to Mugdock if you like."

"I can meet him?" she asked. "This is a true, true story?"

"Aye, I wasn't about to make up another seeing as how disappointed you were the first time."

Agnes put her hand in his and squeezed. Seeing her so happy among her people lightened his heart. There were many dangers ahead of them, but for this night he would do all that he could to keep her the way she was in that moment.

They took their seats as another villager came to tell a tale of a ghostly piper and another of the dreaded kelpies. William looked down from time to time to enjoy watching her watch them. By God, if anyone ever laid a finger on her he would rip them apart with his bare hands. The thought swept through him so fast it surprised him. He didn't just lust after her, he didn't just want to protect her because she was his wife. He loved her. Fully and wholly loved her and the idea of that shocked him.

He'd never given much credence or had any expectation that his marriage would result in love. He had been resigned to have an amicable relationship with a woman he could respect and with whom he could grow a family.

This was unexpected.

After hours of entertainment, the crowd dispersed and William found himself curled in bed next to his perfectly sated and sleeping wife. The evening had been everything he'd hoped it would be and more. Tomorrow, he would tell her of his plan to leave the day following. He hoped she wouldn't be too disappointed, but it was necessary.

Hugh hadn't said much to him after only asking him once how long they would remain. The man would miss his daughter and that was to be expected. William would be pleased to see his home again and his family. His mother was sure to love Agnes.

Love Agnes.

The thought rolled around in his mind again. He'd not unleashed his full passion when they'd come to bed. Rather, he loved her slowly, watching the passion show on her face, staring into her eyes as their bodies joined.

As soon as they returned to Mugdock, he would set about reinforcing his own lands and the castle walls. How he wished there were a faster method to return with her. And then it dawned on him. She could ride in the saddle with him. She would have to wear trews underneath her gown and she would be sore, but galloping with one horse would be faster than waiting for the carriage. He would arrange with Hugh to have some of his men transport the carriage and they could be home much faster. He couldn't harbor the thought of being on the road for more weeks.

William cuddled harder into her and buried his face in her hair. He could stay like this forever with her. Somewhere between a lonely gull cry and the first streak of light entering the chamber, he found light slumber.

In his dreams he fought imaginary foes coming at him from all sides who snatched Agnes from his arms. Try as he might, he could not reach her. No matter what he tried, she remained just out of his grasp. More than once he woke with a start only to fall into the same dream again. By the morning, he was exhausted as though he'd fought the entirety of the Highland rebels and lost everything.

William slid from the bed so as not to wake Agnes. He stood by the window looking out over the sea. In the distance and through the fog he was sure a long tentacle rose from the depths below then slapped hard on the water's surface. Was her sea monster waving farewell, warning of foreboding, or hastening them on their way? He couldn't tell if he was still dreaming or not, but he was sure that much longer in this place and he would lose the last of the wits he had.

CHAPTER THIRTEEN

THEY'D BEEN RIDING for days, and she was ready for the journey to end. While she thoroughly enjoyed being seated in front of William with his strong arms around her and his thick chest pressed against her back, she had to admit her bottom was growing sore.

By day they covered as much ground as possible which meant at night they practically fell from the horse and into whichever inn they could find. He'd kiss her awake before sunrise each morning and pleasure her until she could stand no more. Were it not for the threat and the feeling of looking over their shoulders at all times and her sore arse, she could stay like this with him forever. No time for casually looking about the countryside on this journey. Trees whipped by as they galloped along as fast as they could.

William had arranged for their belongings to follow so she would have only the gown she wore and one other until they reached Mugdock Castle and there she would find plenty of gowns belonging to his sister.

She wanted a bath and a hot meal more than anything, but they did not linger in any one place long enough for either. They'd packed as much as they could carry foodwise so they could eat when the horse needed rest.

They didn't talk much, and she could feel the tension rolling off William, understanding he would not relax until they reached their destination. Thankfully they didn't encounter many travelers either. Only once did he veer off onto a different path when a rider was visible ahead of them.

After she was deliciously woken by him that morning, he had said they would reach the castle that day and she was ready for it. She longed to be off the horse and soaking in a hot tub to ease her muscles. She didn't have time for her nerves to affect her, so at least that was one benefit of their travels. But now as the castle came into view, small flutters entered her belly.

Thrusting up from curtain walls was a tall square tower with several windows dotted across its facade. There was absolutely no way to know what lay beyond unless one entered through the gateway.

William slowed the horse to a trot as they passed through and entered the inner courtyard. He pulled back on the reins and stopped the horse then quickly dismounted. As he reached for her, he shouted at the men guarding the gateway to close the doors. From the inside Agnes could see two heavy wooden doors with thick iron plating holding it together. The men closed the doors then sealed them with a massive wooden beam. Nothing was coming in that way.

A stable hand ran over to William taking the horse away. "Look after him well," he said. "He's had a hard run."

He then turned to Agnes and drew in a deep breath. "I know these past days have been hard on you, but you do understand they were necessary."

"Aye, William, that I do," she said and smiled as the lines in his face began to soften.

"Let's get you inside and out of this heat. I am sure you are hungry and in need of a bath."

He was surely becoming a seer where she was concerned. William took her hand and walked toward a long building adjoining the tower. They entered and walked along a hallway leading to a hall twice the size of her father's. With the enormous hearth at the far end, leading to it was the longest table she'd ever seen. Truly this could rival the king's!

"Welcome to our home," he said to her as he drew her to a woman seated at the head with two younger lads seated on either side.

"William!" the boys exclaimed and ran to him throwing their arms around him.

Agnes stepped to the side and smiled at the sight. It was telling when a man was so free with his affections with siblings. He would make a good father. She hadn't thought about how many children she wanted eventually, but as she watched the elder brother return their embrace, she was convinced more would be merrier.

When the lady approached, William said, "Mother, I would like you to meet my wife, Lady Agnes lately Sinclair, now the Countess of Montrose. Agnes, may I introduce my mother, the Dowager Countess of Montrose."

The lady turned to Agnes with a warm smile that did not quite reach her eyes. There was a melancholy about the woman that made one want to wrap their arms around her and take all her pain away.

"It is lovely to meet you, my lady," she said. Her voice was kind. Agnes liked her immediately.

"It is my pleasure to meet you, my lady, and may I please ask you to call me Agnes."

His mother nodded and smiled at her again. "I am pleased to hear that, and you may call me Mother if it pleases you."

"It does indeed."

"I am pleased with her," she said to William as she embraced him.

The tender way he held his mother made Agnes's heart swell. There was so much she could tell from this brief exchange with his family, and it gave her great comfort.

"And what about us?" one of the boys asked.

"And these are my two impish brothers, Geoffrey and

Glenn." As he said their names he scruffed their hair. The boys pulled away from him only to scruff one another's hair.

"Settle down," his mother said.

The boys listened to their mother, which was refreshing to see. "She's pretty," Geoffrey whispered loudly to Glenn who merely stared at her. Agnes liked them already.

"Now," his mother said, "I am sure by the state of you both you are in need of sustenance. We will get you fed first, and then off to rest. I will keep the meal light this evening, but after that we must plan your nuptial festivities."

"I thank you, mother. We are in need of all that, but we must hold fast on any festivities. There is a reason why we hastened here from Agnes's home."

"What is it?" she asked as her brows drew tight together.

"There is so much to tell you, I hardly know where to begin," he said. William moved past her to take a seat at the table motioning for Agnes to join him.

"Boys! Go tell the cook to bring food and drink."

As they scurried off to do as they were bid, William's mother took her seat and waited. Servants came to clear the table and before long platters of bread, cold meat, and cheese were placed before them. Agnes helped herself and savored every bite while William left out no detail about their time in Stirling, Agnes's uncle, their journey to her home, and the return. His mother listened intently with no interruptions.

"And now we are safely here until we can be sure the threat is no longer a concern. I will speak to our men and secure all entrances, but we must be strict with the boys as they will not be permitted to leave the grounds."

"Were you aware of the threat before you left here for Stirling?" his mother asked.

"Nay. But I learned of it as soon as I arrived. Fin escorted me directly to the king and he divulged his intelligence."

That meant he was aware of her uncle's involvement before she arrived at Stirling. But that would mean—

Agnes felt sick to her stomach. Was their entire meeting a set up? Was he attentive to her because he thought she was a part of the rebel Highlanders? Agnes pushed back her chair and made to stand. She needed some air all of a sudden. Her chest constricted like she was unable to breathe. As soon as she stood, the room spun and she toppled to the floor.

When she woke sometime later, she was on a bed with a coverlet over her. William's mother was by her side quietly working on her needlepoint.

"You gave us quite the fright, lass," she said. "I think I know what troubles you."

How could she possibly know?

"You didn't know he suspected you from the beginning, did you?"

And there it was. Confirmation of the obvious. She had thought he had been drawn to her, but it was him simply performing his duty to his king. Did he care for her now? Aye, she believed he did. But she couldn't help but think their entire connection was built on a lie and she didn't know how to process it.

"Agnes, may I offer some advice?"

"Aye," she whispered.

"Give him a chance to explain himself. He does not know why you're upset or why you had such a reaction to his recount of the events."

"Where is he now?"

"After he brought you up here, he practically shouted down the castle for the village healer. He is gone to fetch her now. God help the woman."

Agnes sat up and swiped a single tear away from her cheek. She would take his mother's advice and speak to him as soon as he arrived. She hated this sick feeling in the pit of her stomach and hoped against hope he had a good explanation.

RACING BACK TO the castle as fast as he could with an elderly lady in tow was not how he wanted to enjoy his first day at Mugdock with Agnes. Christ's teeth, he'd never felt such fear in all his days. As he carried her to his chamber, he whispered to her hoping she could hear his pleas to never leave him. Watching her fall was far more terrifying than anything the Highland rebels could do to him.

They arrived back at the castle, and he helped Old Nan, as everyone called her. She was far spryer than she looked as she walked hastily along with him toward the entrance way.

"This way," he said and led her toward the stairs and onward to his chamber. Inside he found Agnes sitting up and looking pale. He rushed to her and placed his hand on her cheek and winced when she flinched.

"You're awake," he said. "Do you know what happened?"

"I—I just fainted is all."

"Likely from the long journey," Old Nan said and motioned for William to move back.

"Now, child, let me look at you. Move over here closer."

William watched as the woman examined his wife who would not meet his eye. "I will need her to undress," she said. "Would you please step outside, both of you," she said and motioned toward the door with both hands.

Outside his mother placed her hand on his arm. "William, I know what happened, but I think you should hear it from Agnes."

"What is it? You must tell me now."

"I do not want to interfere, but I believe she is only now understanding that you were meant to suspect her before you met her."

That didn't make any sense. "Why would that bother her? She knew of the threat not long after. I made the determination quickly that she was not involved."

"That's not quite the point," she said. "You will need to talk to her. She is upset, and there is only one reason why a person would be that upset."

"And what is that?"

"Ahh, my sweet lad. I will have to let you figure out that one on your own," she said as she turned to leave.

"Where are you going?"

"To have a long talk with my husband. He needs to be reminded of some things."

William shook his head as his mother wandered down the hallway. The place to which she headed was the same spot she took up in the garden each day to have one of her talks with his father. They had made plans to build a bigger marker the previous year, but she would hear none of it. The modest stone was the perfect size, as she was convinced any disturbance would alter the connection between this world and the one beyond where he rested.

The door opened and Old Nan emerged.

"How is she?"

"She will be fine once she is rested."

"Rest? That's all?"

"Aye, laddie. Rest. Now see to it I am returned to my home and in a more peaceful manner. My old bones can't take being bounced around like they used to," she said with a wink.

"Thank you," he said. "You'll find Neville in the hall. He will provide you with your payment and will arrange to get you home. I still think it is time you moved within these walls."

"I am not about to give up my home yet. I thank ye for yer offer and bid thee good day, laddie."

William had known her his whole life and considered her family. He'd been trying for years to build her a home within the castle walls, but she refused. He understood the need for control over one's life and so he left the choice up to her for whenever she might be ready.

He turned to the closed door and lingered for a moment.

Drawing in a deep breath he opened it to find her lying on her side with the covers up to her neck.

"How do you feel?" he asked as he crossed the room and sat on the side of the bed.

Agnes sat up and wrapped her arms around her legs. "I am well."

"You gave me quite the fright."

When she didn't say anything, he realized his mother was right. She was upset, and he wasn't sure how to broach the topic.

"Agnes," he said and faltered. He wasn't quite sure how to put his question into words.

"Were you tasked with becoming close with me to gain intelligence for the king?"

Her question was so abrupt and so harsh when put like that, for a moment or two he could only gaze at her.

"Agnes, it was not like that."

Her gaze locked with his then and she raised her chin. "Then how was it? Fin brought me right to you on that first day in the great hall at Stirling. Right to you," she said and pointed a finger at him. "You cannot convince me that you were unaware of who I was and who my relations were when we first met."

William raked his hands through his hair. She was right. In everything she said. But none of that mattered once he did meet her.

"Very well," he said and stood. "Once I learned of your uncle's possible involvement, I agreed to help discover any person who would pose a threat to the king or the queen. I am loyal to my crown, and I am not ashamed of it."

Agnes turned her head away.

"But all of that was secondary the moment I met you."

Agnes turned back to him but would not meet his gaze.

"Agnes, look at me."

Her gaze slowly lifted to his. He saw sadness and misery behind her eyes. His mother had said there would be a good reason for a person to be this upset over something that no longer mattered between them.

"I remember the moment you walked into the hall with Fin. For a few minutes you did not see me, but I saw you. I watched as this enchanting woman made her way toward me and with each step you took, I fell deeper under your spell. If you were a rebel, I would have been useless to turn you over."

William took her hands into his and squeezed. He was thrilled when she did not pull away.

"I deemed quickly that you were not part of this scheme and that was confirmed when I saw you with your uncle. I believe I fell in love you in that moment, you know?"

Agnes gasped.

"Oh, you didn't know that I am deeply in love with you?" he asked as he tugged her to come closer. "Every moment from the first time I laid eyes on you to now, I have been struck by your honesty, your bravery, your wit, and your charm. I love you, Agnes," he said and softly kissed her lips.

"I love you too," she said and his heart leapt with joy. "But I am hurt that you never told me sooner just how much I was suspected. I am hurt because I thought our first meeting was special and pure and now I don't know how I feel. It's like it's been tainted somehow."

He understood why she felt that way and wasn't sure he could ever change that.

"Agnes, do you know that even if the king had not asked me to meet you and glean what I might know, we would still be right here?"

"What do you mean?"

"I mean you are my other half. Whether you were innocent or guilty, had never been identified to me, I would have still found you, fallen for you, and married you. I do believe we were destined to be together and how we met is of no import now. You are mine and I am yours now and forever. I will never let anything come between us. That I promise you."

She didn't say anything rather crawled onto his lap and placed her head on his chest. He stroked her hair as they sat into a silent truce. If she wanted, he would stay that way with her for all time.

121

CHAPTER FOURTEEN

DID HIS ACCOUNT and his reasoning make sense? Aye. Did she feel like a silly wee lass over how she'd behaved in those first hours with him? Aye. How she would reconcile the two she did not know. The truth of the matter was that they loved one another and that had grown from the beginning; he was right about that. Only time would tell whether or not this new knowledge would continue to bother her. For now, she was in this marriage and she loved this man.

William kissed the top of her head. "I have arranged a bath for you," he said. "The tub will be here shortly, and I have two of the kitchen maids instructed to aid you. You can keep them for your use as long as you wish. Does that suit you, Agnes?"

"Aye," she said. She had no more words for him. And she was glad when he stood up with her in his arms and placed her down upon the bed.

"I must see to security now, but I will check in on you later. And by the way," he said from the door, "this is our chamber and I hope you like it. But if you do not, I will have it furnished to your pleasing."

With that he left the chamber, gently closing the door.

Agnes got up from the bed and moved to the open window. The view overlooked the extensive garden, from beautiful flowers on one side to sculpted bushes and flowering trees on the other side. In the center was a small pond and by it his mother sat near a stone marker. Agnes could faintly hear the woman talking and from time to time soft laughter. The sight was heart wrenching yet comforting at the same time. How would she herself react if something happened to William? Would she go mad with despair or keep his memory alive as his mother did?

The maids came with pails of water and two men carrying a tub. She instructed them to place it by the hearth and turned back to the window as they came back and forth with water until the tub was full.

"My lady, your bath is ready," a quiet voice said from behind her. When she turned, she took in the young women who would tend to her. Agnes was not accustomed to this much devotion but was glad of it, for she was so tired she wasn't sure she could lift her arms to wash her hair.

The two maids were about the same age, by Agnes's guess, barely old enough to serve, yet here they were about to wash a stranger who was now the lady of the castle. It was all a great deal to take in.

"What are your names?"

"I am Alice, and this is Marie," the taller of the two said. "We have brought you some special additions for your bath, m'lady."

"'Tis true," Marie said. "We got it from the kitchen, and they said that a young countess must be treated delicately and that her skin can never become dry. So we brought you all these things," she said as she lifted a cloth to reveal several vials with an oil-like substance in them together with dried lavender and rosehips.

"Will this do, m'lady, or shall we fetch more?"

Agnes smiled. She liked these young ladies.

"This will do quite nicely and since I have only been a countess for a short time, I am not sure what my skin requires. How do you tend the dowager countess?"

They exchanged quick glances. "The dowager countess doesn't want anyone to dote on her. She insists on doing that herself, so we only seldom get to do her hair," Alice said.

"Aye, and we like doing hair," Marie said. "Will you let us do your hair, m'lady?"

"Aye, I will let you do my hair."

She gave over to them entirely. When they had her gown and shift off and helped her into the tub, she felt only a little guilt over being so fawned over.

But she'd been through an ordeal and determined she deserved a little pampering even if she would not indulge on a regular basis. It was nice to know this was available to her. The maids emptied the vials into the steaming water then sprinkled the dried flowers. The scent was magical, as was the way the heat soothed her aching muscles. She didn't realize just how sore she was until the bath water touched each and every part of her.

Agnes lay back with her hair hanging over the back of the tub after they fully washed and rinsed it. The maids lifted her limbs and gently washed her from one end to the other only handing her the cloth to handle her more private areas.

The heat combined with the soft scent wafting around her and the gentle brushing drew her toward slumber. She was just starting to drift when one of the maids touched her shoulder.

"M'lady, 'tis time for you to get out now. Too much time in there might make your skin wrinkly."

Agnes smiled to herself. She'd had *wrinkly* skin from a long bath before. That was a sign it had been a good one, but nonetheless, she would get out and then maybe explore the grounds while William was away. She was tired, but she was more curious about her new home.

The maids helped her out of the tub and into a modest pale-blue satin gown once she was dried. It was one of the ones William had promised her, having previously belonged to his sister, Elspeth.

"This looks far better on you than it ever did on *her*," Alice said and then clapped her hand over her mouth as if realizing the seriousness of her statement.

"I am sorry, m'lady. Sometimes my mouth speaks my

thoughts before I can stop them."

"You will get us both into trouble with that mouth of yours," Marie said.

Agnes was curious and so did not scold them. "You do not like Lady Elspeth?" When neither of them spoke, she said, "I promise your words are safe in my ears. I do not condone gossip, but you may tell me this one time and then we will forget all about it." Agnes waited until finally Alice spoke up.

"She was spoiled and had a way of being kind when the earl was around and then mean when he was not. If he only knew the vicious things she did."

"What kind of things?" Agnes asked.

"If she lost something or broke something, she would always blame the boys."

"Aye, those two sweet little boys, who never did anything other than the impish things little boys do, took more than one trimmin' because of her. We were all glad when she married and finally left."

"And now you are here and we can tell right away you are a good person, and you will be a good countess too. We can tell."

"Aye," Marie said, nodding her head. "We can tell."

"Well, thank you both very much. And as I said, your words are safe with me, but I would advise you not to repeat them to anyone else, lest you find yourselves in trouble."

They both nodded and then ushered her to a chair to work on her hair. Much time and anecdotes about the boys later, Agnes was ready to explore the castle on her own. With William off for the rest of the day seeing to his business, she was first curious about the gardens as it was still only late afternoon and would be warm for a few hours yet.

She left the maids to attend to removing the bath and clearing away the chamber and made her way back to the great hall. A man was inside and made eye contact with her the moment she entered. He came forward with a beaming smile. He took her hand and kissed the back of it then bowed.

"Lady Graham, it is a pleasure to meet you. I am Neville, the earl's steward, and yours now too."

She liked him immediately. He was about her father's age and had a kind face. Tall and muscular, he must have been hard on the ladies in his younger days.

"The pleasure is mine, Neville. I was about to find my way around to explore the gardens," she said.

"Say no more," he said. "William asked me to show you around should you wish while he is attending to some things in the village."

She took his offered arm and walked with him outside and away from the hall and the gateway. The air was still with only the sound of a lonely hawk off in the distance. She glanced once more at the gateway and put William from her mind.

WILLIAM MOUNTED HIS horse and trotted along the path leading from the tanner to the blacksmith. He'd need some additional weapons, and he didn't need them to be perfect, he just needed them sharp. Word had come from the king the rebels had indeed set their sight on Agnes in retaliation for John Sinclair.

He was sick to his stomach as he didn't know how or when they would strike, but he needed to put his plan into motion straight away. She was probably still upset with him, but he hoped in time she would see the seriousness of the situation and the truth of his words.

"How long will it take for this order?" he asked Riley the blacksmith once he listed out his items. Long swords, daggers, and axes. Their armory was well stocked with arrows, but they were low on the other items, and he intended to put a weapon in every man's hand.

"If I bring on my apprentices, three days, and they will be long days at that."

"Do what you can," he said and placed a bag of coin on the anvil. "Buy what you need. And if you see anyone around you don't recognize, do not engage with them. Keep to your business and stay out of harm's way. I'll send Neville in three days to collect what you've completed. And I am sending extra men to keep watch out in the village. You are in no danger here. They're not looking for anyone here."

"Aye, m'lord."

William left the blacksmith and headed over to the inn. He told them much the same as he'd told Riley. Stay inside, stay safe, and keep an eye out. And that was the best he could do. He'd offered any and all of them refuge behind the castle walls, but they all one by one refused, stating they feared no Highlander and they would take their chances in their own homes.

"Let them come," Old Nan said. "I'll show them a thing or two about loyalty."

William smiled at her spunk. She was a force to be reckoned with, and he had no doubt she would find a way to defend herself.

By the time he made his rounds, the sun was just beginning to set. He mounted his horse and headed for Mugdock Castle. He took the faster main path, though he realized he'd be exposed. Not long after leaving the village he passed through a copse of trees and upon emerging on the other side, felt the woosh of an arrow pass by his left shoulder. William kicked in his heels hard and leaned forward, willing the horse to gallop faster.

Another arrow whooshed by him grazing his skin. The thunder of hooves behind him grew louder and as the gates of the castle came into view, he shouted for the men to open the gate. Just as he made his way inside, two arrows found their mark, one in his shoulder and one in his thigh. The gates closed behind him and as he slowed the horse, the courtyard spun so quickly, he lost his balance and slid from his horse.

The sky was an orangey pink with soft white clouds. His body floated toward them. He closed his eyes grimacing against the hot burning pain searing his broken flesh. No normal arrow would do this. They must have been tipped, but with what he could not tell. And would have no time to say anything. His tongue thickened in his mouth, as something wet dripped down his cheek.

Agnes.

He'd promised her he'd be safe. That nothing would happen to him. He opened his eyes again to see his guardsmen above him. One reached for the arrow and the other swiped his hand away.

"Thipped," he whispered.

"We know," one of them said. "Don't talk. We will get you inside and cleaned up."

"Agneth," he whispered trying to tell them to keep her safe.

He closed his eyes again as the pain raged through his body. He knew of a few poisons favored for tipping arrows, the worst being nightshade. He prayed it was something lesser and that they could help him in time. That he had not lost consciousness was promising. Perhaps they meant it as a warning and to scare him.

His body was lifted onto something hard. Many people shouted around him as he opened and closed his eyes trying to stay awake. The pain in his shoulder and thigh had gotten so bad it threatened to make him lose his guts.

Once in the great hall he recognized they had placed him on the table. Neville entered then and that was when he saw her. The horror on her beautiful face when she spied the state of him was something he would never forget. She ran to him and took his hand into hers.

He tried to speak but no words would form as another wave of pain ripped through him. Agnes squeezed his hand and mopped his brow with a cloth. From where she'd found it, he did not know. His shirt was ripped off as was one side of his trews. So many people were yelling and he just wanted to sleep. He couldn't understand what they wanted of him.

Finally, one person's words got through.

"You will not break your promise to me," Agnes said. "Do you hear me? You will not die on me."

He tried to nod, but the pain was unbearable. It hurt to think. There was no way he could speak.

"William, look at me," she said as she shook him. "Look at me!"

He opened his eyes and stared into her beautiful tear-filled eyes gazing back at him with so much fear and pain. He wanted to replace it with joy and happiness. He had to fight this evil raging through his body, and he would do it for her!

"William, they have to remove the arrow. Keep your focus on me. I am here with you and will see you through this."

Barely able to comprehend her words, he saw black when they pulled the arrow through his shoulder. Something wet splattered across his face then he felt a great pressure above and below his shoulder. Agnes mopped his brow again. He couldn't tell if he was bathed with sweat or blood. But what had landed in his mouth was metallic, signifying the latter.

"One more, William," Agnes said. "Look at me again, William. Hold my hand tighter, as tight as you can."

He was as weak as a kitten. He tried to do as she asked, but his strength left him as fast as the blood pouring from him.

When they pulled the next arrow through, he saw stars. And not the pleasant kind he'd seen when overcome with pleasure. These burst behind his eyes, and he turned his head and retched to the side away from his wife.

More pressure on his thigh and shoulder left him hanging on by a thread.

"That's good. You did it, William. You will recover now. Aye, keep pressure hard on both wounds," she said to someone else. Then back to him, "We have to move you now, William. We will be as gentle as we can, but you have to stay awake. You have to listen to my voice and stay awake. Do you understand?"

The next sound he heard was his mother's shrieks.

"No. No. No," she screamed as they passed by to make their way to his chamber. His eyes opened and closed as he held Agnes's hand, focusing on the sound of her voice.

She cooed to him, praising his bravery and strength. She told him she loved him and that she would not leave his side no matter what. He believed her. And he believed she loved him. That one thing would see him through. He would fight this, and he would survive to grow old with her and have many bairns. That was the life he was supposed to have, the life he would have, and nothing, no damned rebel would take that from him.

William turned his head to look at her as they placed him on his bed and servants came in with water and cloths to clean his wounds. True to her word, Agnes did not leave his side and gently stroked his forehead with a damp cloth. People came in and out of the chamber, but he kept his focus on her.

Slowly after a time the pain eased a little and his body relaxed; she urged him to drink a cup of something warm and bitter, and within a short time slumber creeped upon him. He fell into a deep sleep with his wife by his side not knowing if he'd ever wake.

CHAPTER FIFTEEN

S HE ENDURED A hellish night. William had developed a high fever and no amount of cool cloths would bring it down. Somewhere after midnight the old lady who insisted to be called Nan arrived with a satchel filled with different vials and bunches of dried plants. Her bag of tricks, she'd called it. Neville had left for the village not long after they'd settled William into their chamber. He told her that the chamber and the castle would be guarded and to let no one except for him and the old lady enter.

Agnes helped Nan mix and stir her ingredients all the while the old lady singing old tunes Agnes had never heard. Old Gael's tunes, she told her while they tried to position William so they could pour some in his mouth. He spurted and sputtered, but eventually managed to get two cups of the mixture that oddly had little smell into him.

"And now we wait," Nan said.

They did wait and somewhere around dawn his fever finally broke, and they were able to roll him so they could change the soaked bed covers and put on fresh.

Agnes was exhausted. Nan had fallen asleep in the chair by the hearth despite Agnes insisting on finding her a bed. She wanted to be close when William awoke as according to her, he would have a nasty headache from the poison for a few hours.

Agnes lay down beside him and though his fever had broken,

his skin was still hot to the touch, as if the poison clung to him, unyielding in its purpose. She closed her eyes and tried to sleep, but images of him with arrows sticking out of his shoulder and thigh would give her no peace. She rolled over to her side and put her arm across his chest hoping the steady thud of his heart would settle her.

After a time she finally dozed, but only for a few minutes before William started shaking. She got up to get a cloth, and Nan woke at the same time.

"Time to mix the next set of tonics, lass."

While Nan pulled other plants from her satchel, Agnes mopped William's brow. She hated this. Hated seeing him in such a state. And she hated not having full understanding of the true danger surrounding them.

Neville knocked and entered just as they were pouring more mixture into William's mouth. This tincture reeked of something rotten. Thankfully, though he choked on it a little, he swallowed it.

"He will sleep now for the rest of the day and by then the poison will have run the worst of its course," Nan said. "Now I'll take that bed."

"I have it already arranged," Neville said. "Tell Connor outside to bring you to the white room."

After she left, Neville turned to Agnes. "The king has sent many guards to ensure our safety."

"But how did he know we were attacked?"

"William had anticipated such and instructed one of the guards in your party to travel to Stirling instead of here with a missive and a request for added protection."

"He hadn't told me that."

"He didn't want you to worry."

"But I had good reason, didn't I?" The stress of the last several hours welled within her, threatening to spill over. She didn't want to unleash it on Neville, but he was unfortunately the only one present at the moment to whom she could vent.

"My lady, protecting his family is his lordship's highest priority."

"I understand that, but in doing so it is he who has been fighting for his life on that bed."

Agnes clenched and unclenched her fists. She was tired of everyone around her making decisions having a direct impact on her without her consult or awareness.

"I am sorry, my lady. Is there anything I can have brought to you?"

"Aye, a platter of food and mead, and the same for Nan. And I want parchment, ink, quill, and wax seal."

Neville tilted his head to the side, but thankfully said nothing. She expected him to obey her without question. He was not familiar enough with her to challenge her. She was finished with letting everyone else work on solutions and, by God, she would take matters into her own hands. She was the one who'd traveled to Stirling with her uncle. She could have forewarned Fin, the queen, and William. But she had been so enchanted by the king's court and William that she'd focused on her own childish desires rather than the safety and protection of others.

She'd brought the devil to court.

And she would remedy this business if it was the last thing she ever did.

Neville returned with all the items she had requested and quietly waited. Good. He knew his place and that pleased her and made her respect him all the more. After she broke her fast, she sat down to write her own missive.

Your Honorable Majesty;

I write to you in good faith to express my sincerest thanks for your kindness to us in sending your guards for our protection. Your generosity is unmatched, as is your grace. I share with you, the earl has succumbed to injury due to poisoned arrows in his shoulder and thigh. He has weathered the poison and will heal in full according to the healer who attended him. I ask one further favor of you. Would you kindly spare one of your surgeons to come see to him to ensure his limbs will sustain no permanent damage. I fear that expertise may lie beyond our healer. I also wish to inform you, I am writing a missive to your wife to continue my friendship with her as I am hopeful I am no longer suspected of treason. I humbly await your reply,

Your faithful servant,
Agnes Montrose

Anges folded the letter and sealed it then pulled new parchment to start her next letter.

Your Honorable Majesty, my dear friend;

I have informed His Majesty of my husband's injury and that of his expected recovery and thanked him for the extra protection. But I write to you for a different reason. As soon as my husband has proven he is no longer in mortal danger, it is my intention to travel to you in order to speak with my uncle to plead with him to order the immediate cessation of attacks on those under royal protection. I am certain with my persistence we can resolve this matter once and for all. I kindly await your reply and am hopeful of your compliance to my request.

Your faithful servant and friend,
Agnes Montrose

She folded her second letter and sealed it in the same manner as the first. Once done, she handed both to Neville.

"Have these sent to the palace in the safest and fastest manner possible. I wish the rider to wait for a reply."

Neville looked confused for a moment as he looked down at the letters and then to her as well. "My lady, do you wish to consult with me regarding the content of the letters?"

"There is no need for you to worry, Neville. While you're thinking about the safest and fastest way to do as I ask, also devise a way that you may offer the same way for me to travel there as well, as soon as I am sure my husband's peril has passed."

Neville looked over at William and back to her and shook his head. He looked positively mortified. "My lady, I don't think—"

Agnes put her hand up. "I am not asking you to think. I am asking you to do two things and do them well. I have a lot riding on both and I assure you, your laird will not blame you for my actions. I will see to it with my third letter. Now go. Twenty miles is a long distance, and I will not rest until a reply is returned."

To his credit, he left the chamber immediately. The sun was still low in the sky so she would wait to speak to Nan to find out how long it would be before William woke and would be aware. If he knew of her plan, he would forbid it, and she couldn't let that happen.

Nay, she must get to her uncle and convince him she was a supporter. That was the only way she could acquire the intelligence the king needed to put a stop to all this madness.

Agnes took another piece of parchment and dipped the quill in the ink then hesitated. How much of her plan would she reveal to him? Would that put him in more danger? She had to tell him something so his anger would not be misplaced onto Neville. But she did not want him tearing off to ruin her plot. She could do this.

My dearest husband;

WILLIAM WAS SOMEWHERE between heaven and hell each time he woke. He was either racked with pain and fever or he floated along on some cloud where his sense of touch had completely disappeared as though he did not possess a body. How much time had passed since his injury he could not say but each time he woke, Agnes was by his side tending to him and cooing sweet words.

He would regain his strength and do everything in his power

to make them safe again, so they did not need to live like they were in their own self-made prison.

William woke with a start and immediately searched the bed for Agnes. He sat up and looked around the dark chamber. A fire burned low in the hearth, and someone sat by the fire with white hair spilling over the back. He whipped back the covers and swung his long legs down to the floor. The movement made everything around him spin and he fell back onto the bed holding his head with his hands. A low pounding started at the base of his skull. He closed his eyes to dull it.

"Now, now. You are not ready to be out of bed yet. The poison will hurt your head for a few days yet, so you need to rest."

He knew the voice immediately. The bed covers were pulled up over him as she said, "Here you must drink this. 'Tis not pleasant, but it will aid the pain in your head."

He opened his eyes and took the cup from Old Nan. He drank the liquid which tasted like rotten meat, but he downed it anyway as he trusted her as much as anyone.

"Where is my wife?"

"You need not worry about her now," she said. "Wait a minute and the tonic will help with your head."

William sat up though his head started spinning again.

"You should lay down again, laddie. You could hurt yourself in your state."

Her words were foggy and she became blurred to him. William lay down as he had no strength to do otherwise. "Tell me where is Agnes?" he whispered.

"Shh, sleep now, laddie."

William fell into a deep sleep. He dreamed he was in a thick wood with dozens of pathways, some lighted and some dark. He searched and searched, but he could not find her. After what seemed like fruitless hours, he discovered a path brighter than the others. Something sparkled along this one, so he followed the path, which led to a brightly moonlit meadow. All sorts of frost-covered flowers swayed to and fro in the soft breeze as if in some sort of death dance.

In the middle of the clearing, he found them.

Cailleach stood tall holding Agnes, her icy staff pointing at her throat.

"I wondered when you'd find us," the crone said in a raspy voice.

"Let her go," he said in the strongest voice he could, though his body was still weak.

"And what do I get if I release her?"

"You get to live," he said. He meant it. He'd rip her apart with his bare hands if he had to.

"William, I'm sorry," Agnes said. "It was the only way."

"What do you mean?"

"She means she has come here of her own free will, offering herself to me in order to save you."

"Agnes, no!"

"Aye," the crone said with a cackle. "I win after all these years. I will either get a mortal body in the form of you or of her."

"You will get neither; now, release her!"

"Or what?" the crone asked. "What power do you have over me?"

"William, please. You will live and be strong and the fighting will end. She will destroy the rebels for us."

"You don't need to do this, Agnes. I will find the rebels. I will destroy them."

"You cannot; you were harmed. I cannot stand by and see you suffer like that. It was killing me."

"Agnes, I cannot live without you."

"But you will live," she said. "The most important thing is that you will live." As she said this, a single tear fell down her cheek. "I love you with all my heart and soul and I make this sacrifice for you."

The crone tilted her head back and let out a loud wicked

laugh. "She is mine!"

She drew her staff away from Agnes and made to plunge it into her neck just as William lunged forward. As he was about to knock the staff from her hands, they disappeared before him. NO!

William searched the meadow. Little by little the frost faded from the flowers and their colors returned. The moonlight dulled as clouds passed over its brightness. All color and light continued to fade until there was only blackness. William did not know how long he stood alone in the black with only the sound of his ragged breathing and his pounding heartbeat to comfort him.

He had to get away from this dark place—this hell hole. He needed to get back to the light to where Agnes was, where they loved one another and would make their family.

William turned around and around but could not find anything on which to aim his gaze. An eon later he noticed a small pinhole of light coming through from a distance. He ran toward it and as he did it grew larger. Shapes formed within the light, trees now and a road were visible. Faster and faster he ran toward it and just as he was about to reach it, he found himself falling away from it. He reached and grabbed and tried to find footing, but he fell so hard and fast that the light faded back to a pinhole and then to nothing.

William woke with a start and sat up to find his bearings. The pain in his head was nearly gone, and the room was so bright his eyes hurt.

"Hush, laddie. You are safe. I will get you your medicine now."

"Nay," he said. "No more medicine. I will take the headache. That stuff makes me feel odd in my head."

"As you wish, laddie. But it is here if you need it."

William blinked and ran his hands through his hair. He felt like shite. "How long have I been like this?"

"Four nights, and this is your fifth day."

He looked around the chamber to see it all neat and tidy.

Only the side table with her medicine ingredients was a little cluttered. He turned his attention to the empty spot beside him. "Where is my wife?"

"I had better fetch Neville," she said and made her way to the door.

William was still reeling from the terrible dream he'd had. By God, what was in that tincture that made him dream like that? It has been so vivid!

Something was wrong. He could sense it, knowing it was not just left-over emotion from his dream.

Neville knocked then entered the chamber. "I am glad to see the whites of your eyes," he said.

"Aye, I am glad they can be seen."

"How do you feel?"

"Like I've been poisoned." His attempt at a jest didn't register on Neville's face. "Where is my wife?"

"Do you want water brought for a bath? Food?"

Why would no one answer his question? "Neville, aye I want all of those things. But mostly I want my wife."

Neville sighed and pulled something from his pocket then passed it to him.

William took the missive and broke the seal. He opened it and read.

My dearest husband;

I have sat beside you while you fought your battle with the poison. Nan is a wonderful healer and assures me you will make a full recovery, but will be in and out while the poison leaves your body and you recover your strength from your wounds.

I have decided to seek permission from the queen and king to see my uncle. I believe I can convince him to do the right thing and reveal to me who these rebels are and how to track them down. I promise you I will take every precaution for my safety, as I am certain will Neville and the king. Do not be vexed with me. I cannot stand by and let these events unfold without taking action. I believe I can get through to my uncle. I will make this right.

Yours lovingly,
Agnes

Jesus in the garden, she was going to get herself killed. "Ready my horse," he said to Neville.

"He is already set for you, my lord. As is mine."

"How could you let her go?"

William regretted his words the moment they left his mouth. Neville would not have the power to stop his lady.

"I assure you, she arrived safely at Stirling and was delivered directly to the king."

Well, there was that at least.

"You must eat something before we travel," Neville said. "You are not fit in this state."

William couldn't really argue with him. He was hungry, and a wash wouldn't go astray.

"Very well, I will eat and clean myself up, and then we will ride. Is that acceptable?"

"Aye, my lord. I do not want any harm to come to either of you."

"I know that, Neville. I know."

William flicked the sheets off him and stood. He was a little rocky, but he felt better than he had in days. He wondered what in all that was holy would possess her to take such a risk. Once he caught up to her, he didn't know if he would embrace her in relief or tan her hide. Or maybe both.

CHAPTER SIXTEEN

PULLING DOWN HER hood only when she was securely in the presence of the king and queen, Agnes drew in a deep breath and curtseyed.

"I thank you, Your Majesties."

"Sit. I am certain you are travel weary," the queen said and motioned to a chair at their table. "I have food and drink prepared for you and a bed when you are ready."

"Truly, you did not have to wait up so late for me," she said, but was glad to see them. The journey had been uneventful as they had disguised her as much as they could having dressed her in trews and a tunic all covered by a hooded cape.

"Am I to adopt this new fashion of yours?" the queen asked.

Agnes looked down at her attire and couldn't help but smile. "I would appreciate it if I could borrow a gown before I see my uncle," she said. If it all went wrong, she would need to travel through dangerous territory once again and she wouldn't want them to expect her falsehood.

Agnes accepted the food and drink. She was ravenous and the activity helped settle her nerves. Entering into a battle of wits with her uncle was no small feat. He was a determined and clever man who was without his freedom now for some weeks. There was no way to tell what his demeanor would be like or if he would trust her.

"About this business," the king said. "Why do you take on this burden? Your uncle is a dangerous man and can be quite conniving."

"I traveled here with my uncle and half listened to his ramblings for days on end. I should have paid closer attention and understood the danger of his stories and alerted you the moment I arrived. I did not do that and aye, I know I am not responsible for his actions, but I do feel a sense of duty in that I might have prevented the harm that had been intended for you and which has come upon my husband."

"You are under no obligation to put yourself in harm's way. He is secure in a prison cell, and we are closing in on the rebels as we speak."

"I am glad to hear that, but I might glean some new information that would aid in that endeavor."

"I see," he said. "How do you plan to convince him to give up his allies?"

She had hoped he would not ask that question. Agnes could not lie to the king to his face. That would be treason. That she'd done so in writing was bad enough. More falsehoods from her and he would no doubt put her right in the cell with Uncle John.

"I haven't really thought about exactly what I would say," she said. That was one truth at least.

The king watched her carefully and stroked his chin. "Do you plan to convince him to give up the other rebels as you say? Or do you have something else planned?"

"Aye." Another truth. He would give up the rebels when he was sure that she was on his side. And aye, that was the other thing she had planned.

"Aye, to which, Lady Montrose? You are speaking to your king, now. You may lie to your husband, but you may not lie to me."

The warning shot was fired across the bow and she would tread lightly. "Your Majesty, 'tis my intention to extract information from my uncle to aid you in finding these traitors and bringing them to justice."

"Aye, you said that in your letter in not so many words. I understand that. But how will you do that? Your uncle has not responded to my questioning. What makes you think he will respond to your plea?"

And there it was. The direct question for which she could not answer in a cryptic way.

She drew in a deep breath. "Because I will convince him I have seen his path and am now loyal to him and his cause."

The queen gasped. "If I had known you were going to attempt something like that, I would not have let you come. That is a dangerous game to play, Agnes."

"I appreciate your concerns, truly I do. But I know my uncle. I know what to say to convince him he can trust me."

"You are certain you are up to this task?" the king asked.

She wasn't, but she could think of no other way to resolve the problem and keep everyone safe. Though they were her king and queen, she felt a kinship with both of them in the time she'd spent in their company.

"Then it is set. I will make orders that you be escorted to his cell in the morning. For tonight, my wife will have the servants attend you and show you to your chamber."

"Thank you, Your Majesty. You are both very kind."

She finished her meal and bid them good night. Now in the chamber she'd been offered when she first arrived at Stirling Castle, she stared up at the canopy above. How much had changed since she first encountered this view. How much she had changed. Now a married woman and involving herself in a plot to uncover a deadly threat against the king and queen. It was like something out of a story one would tell at a feast. She smiled. Perhaps she would tell it to her children one day. She rubbed her belly. She didn't think she was with child yet, but in her heart, she was certain she would be, and soon. Sometimes one just knew these things. She closed her eyes and tried to find slumber.

On the morrow, she would pull every ounce of courage she

could muster, and she would prove her own loyalty. That to her family and her king and queen. She would make them all proud. Her thoughts drifted to her parents. What wouldn't they do to protect those they loved? Her father thought them safe at Girnigoe, but she was convinced they would only be safe when this threat had ended. And the only way to do that was to remove it.

Agnes turned to her side, anxious she couldn't find sleep. She shaped and reshaped the pillow, but that comfortable spot eluded her. She turned to her other side and found the same problem. She sat up and smoothed the side where her husband should be. He would be vexed at first, but once she delivered true results, he would have to concede the point that her solution was sound.

Pulling the heavy pillows from the other side of the bed, she positioned them as if a body lay beside her. She pulled up the covers and flung an arm and a leg around it and pulled it tight to her body. Agnes buried her head in the pillow and breathed deeply. The scent was fresh and she envisioned it was him. The thought brought her comfort. She closed her eyes and let her mind drift to some of the beautiful moments they had shared. In her mind's eye, she pictured his smiling face with deep dimples and those bright eyes. His delicious mouth that did all sorts of pleasurable things to her. The sound of his groans as his pleasure overtook him. She let her mind pull on all the wonderful and delightful moments that had passed between them.

He was her world now. She could have never imagined finding someone like him and the love they shared. He loved her and she loved him and nothing, no uncle, no rebel, would ever take that away from them or threaten it ever again.

Thoughts of the joy he'd brought her were then replaced with raw determination to see her plan to fruition. Aye, she would succeed. She had to. She would not risk her safety otherwise, for she did not take this action lightly. She would make this right.

THOUGH HER MOTIVES might have been pure, Agnes had no right to tear off to face this business on her own until he was in a better state to handle it. And he had every intention to handle it as soon as he prevented her from speaking to her uncle. The man was the devil's spawn, and who knew how he might manipulate her? Och, he couldn't get to her fast enough.

He was grateful for Neville's care of him for the man had been correct. If William had not filled his belly, there was no doubt he'd never make the journey in one piece. Now with the castle in sight, he kicked his heels hard and his horse took off in an even faster gallop. The only precaution he'd taken was to take two of the king's guards with him who had done their best to keep up with him.

William entered through the gateway and slid of his horse, tossing the reins to a stable boy who ran up immediately.

As he entered the hall, Fin met him in the doorway. "Where is she?"

"She is meeting with her uncle," he said wearing a rather pale pallor. "The king is in his apartment and bids you join him there."

"He is not even there with her?"

"Nay, he said after he spoke with her last evening, it was better she go with the guards herself."

What the hell was going on? He would not break a direct order from the king, but by God this was folly! She was in very real danger.

He followed Fin to where the king sat with his legs outstretched with his hands behind his head. To anyone unaware, one would swear the man had not a care in the world.

"My wife, Your Majesty," William said.

"Is meeting with her uncle and you look like death warmed over."

"Aye, Fin told me that. How long has she been down there?"

"She's been there a while now and should be returned to me soon."

"Why did you let her go by herself?"

The king's eyes narrowed. "You don't approve?"

"Nay, I do not, Your Majesty. I believe John Sinclair to be vile and conniving. I do not feel she is safe in any way in his company."

"You doubt your king's ability to keep his people safe under his own roof?"

"Nay, Your Majesty. I am more convinced of his ability to control a young lady."

"Ahhh, there it is."

"I do not understand."

"Well, first of all sit, before you fall."

William did as he was bid and accepted the goblet of ale offered him. He sipped the liquid and was pleased by the coolness of the drink after his long and strenuous ride.

"Your young wife is not so fragile as you might think," he said with a smirk.

"What does that mean?"

"It means she has hatched a rather clever plot of her own and if successful will be quite the ruse."

William was utterly confused. Didn't she come here to plead with her uncle? "I confess, I do not share your knowledge of this plot."

"Your darling wife, it would appear, has determined she can convince her uncle that she is now loyal to him and use that to extract useful information from him."

"What?"

"Aye. 'Tis rather brilliant. And before you jump to any conclusion, nay, I do not believe her to be a mole."

William had difficulty wrapping his thoughts around what the king said. Agnes intended to outsmart her uncle? Of all the imaginings he'd run through in his mind of what he'd find when he arrived there, this was not one of them.

"She will gain his trust in some way and what then—he will just willingly give up the rebels' hiding place?"

"She is convinced that is the case."

"And you believe she can do this?"

"I believe it is a chance worth taking. My spies have watched comings and goings, but have not yet pieced together a definitive gathering place. And they would alternate meeting places; that only makes sense. But there would have to be somewhere they crafted the poison arrows that pierced you together with other weapons. These wasps have a nest, of that I'm certain. If she can uncover it, 'twill be an incredible boon for us. We could remove this threat for good."

William sat back and took it all in. His head and his body hurt. While he was still concerned for her safety, he had to give her credit. The idea was a clever one. He just wished she had waited until he had awoken to discuss it with him so they could have devised the plan together. And now all he could do was wait.

"How many guards are with her?"

"Six."

William shook his head and crossed his arms over his chest. "This will not work."

"And why is that?"

"He won't open up to her with the guards present."

"Ahhh, but you see that is where you are wrong."

"What else have you not told me?"

"She has written to him and brought quill, ink, and parchment with her. The guards have been instructed to not notice."

"Did you read this letter she will pass him?"

"Aye, I have. She is quite good with words, you know. I filled in any blanks in the story she wanted to recount to ensure he believes her. That is why she has not yet returned, I am almost certain of it."

William grew more wary by the moment. He stood to pace the room. So much could go wrong with this plot. If she was successful, would she later regret so thoroughly betraying a family member? She could not have completely thought this through.

"You still have doubts."

"Aye, many. What if the information he gives her is false?"

"Then we are no better off but no worse either."

"Nay, we *are* worse off. The bounty on my wife's head grows, and we will never be at peace."

Christ's teeth, every moment she remained in his company she was in more danger. He had to put an end to this madness right now.

William stood. "Your Majesty, only a direct order from you will stop me from leaving this room and seeking out my wife to remove her from that place."

"You may go to her, as I believe she will be close to finished by now. But do not imperil what she may have accomplished unless she is in serious danger."

"Aye, Your Majesty. Thank you."

Serious danger be damned. If she was even close to wee danger he'd remove her from it. He left the room to find Fin outside waiting.

"Will you see me to the prison cell holding John Sinclair?"

"Aye, my lord. This way."

Fin turned and led the way through the apartment wing and outside to another section of the castle, then down many winding stairs to a tall, locked gate. A fat man with many keys emerged from the side and opened the gate to allow them entrance.

"On down to the last cell, then turn left and he is down at the far right, last cell down. The king didn't want him to ever overhear anyone else speaking lest he get a secret message out through another prisoner. Mind yerselves. There's bad men in this place." As he said the last words and the door clanged shut, he whistled and walked away.

The stench was almost unbearable of shite and vomit and piss. He didn't want his Agnes anywhere near this place or these men. Imperil her plan or not, she was leaving here as soon as he found her. This place was unclean for one such as she, and he would never allow such a feat to occur again. She was his wife and he would protect her with his life. This situation with the rebels was not hers to fix. She was in no way answerable for their actions or his injury. And by God, if anyone were to lay a hand on her he would tear them asunder.

As they passed by the cells, the men reacted and by the time they reached the end of the first hallway, howls had erupted from the cells. Some called out curses and others yelled, "They're coming." William could not get this business done with fast enough. Fin looked like he was about to lose his guts and his wits.

"Steady," William said to him. "We will get her out of here. I will stay out of sight. You go to her and tell her the king bids her back."

"Aye, my lord."

It would be all over soon.

CHAPTER SEVENTEEN

WATCHING HIM CAREFULLY as he read her note, Agnes prayed he would take the bait. His brows drew in tight as he read her words, flipped the parchment to see if there was any writing on the back and then read it again. Iron bars separated them in this cell which was used for questioning. The guards had removed him from his normal cell which had a wooden door and one slot to view a prisoner by sliding the metal closure. They'd placed a stool opposite the entry for her to sit advising her to keep her distance.

Once they turned their backs, she slipped him the note and waited. The stench of the place was such that she wouldn't be able to stay too long lest she lose her guts all over herself. In her note she recounted some of the phrases he'd used and referred to some of the stories to illustrate her loyalty. She signed the letter with *Loyalty is Everything, Agnes.*

After what seemed like an age, he looked at her and smiled with his brows raised. She nodded and forced a smile in return. She slipped quill, ink, and parchment beneath the iron door meant for food and pointed to it.

He took it and immediately sat and began his reply. He scribbled quickly, often looking up to see if the guards watched him.

"How are you being treated?" she asked him. He looked a state. His clothes were dirty and he was unkempt, which was in stark contrast to how he'd been before.

"They're feeding me well," he said. "But the lodgings are much to be desired. My requests for a daily bath have gone unanswered. Maybe you could put in a word for me?"

"Aye, Uncle, I will see what I can do."

"Tell me why you have come as you know of the accusations against me."

"I have come to plead and reason with you to cease this business and hand over the other rebels of this senseless cause."

Of course, their talk was only for show to convince him she lied for the guards' sake. Her letter had told him that much as well.

"You do not think me foolish enough to cease now we have come so far. I may be captured, but they will never find the rest for we are spread far and wide."

"My husband has been injured, and they will not stop until I am as well, or worse. Do you not have any sense of loyalty to me and to our family?"

"It is to honor our family that I will not back away from this cause. Not for you nor anyone else. I will see this through 'til the end."

John's eyes narrowed as he lifted the folded parchment to hand it to her. A moment of hesitation and he withdrew his hand. "You are not being false with me, are you, niece?" he asked in a low voice.

"Whatever do you mean? I am come to plead with you to withdraw. There is nothing false in that."

He took out the letter she'd given him again and read it once more. Then looked her up and down. "You do not look like you've been mistreated," he murmured.

Agnes could see her plot unraveling before her. She had to think of something and quickly for she could hear footfalls approaching. This might be her only chance. She had to get the letter he'd written as she was convinced it contained vital information.

Rushing to the bars she held on to them and whispered, "Someone is coming. I am out of time and need your help. Please, Uncle. That information is vital to my safety. I won't live without it."

He hesitated and then passed her his note. Agnes took it and tucked it into the pocket in her skirt and then retreated to the stool.

"I take it you will not bend, then, Uncle? You will not order your rebel friends to cease their traitorous activity?"

"I will not."

"My lady," Fin said. "The king orders you away from the prisoner now."

She had to keep up the act for just a few more minutes. "Very well, Fin. I will go with you. But I insist my uncle be treated better than he has. He has requested fresh water to bathe, and he should be permitted that much as he is my relative." Then to John she said, "Farewell, Uncle. I am disappointed I could not make you see reason. Your fate is now out of my hands."

With that she walked past Fin, past the guards, and onward toward the end of the hall to make the turn. When she did, she ran straight into William's chest. The stench of the prison was swiftly replaced with his scent of leather and the outdoors. A loud "Oh!" escaped her lips to which William put his finger to his lips.

"What is happening?" John called from the cell. "What are you doing to my niece?"

"I am well, Uncle, I merely tripped over my gown."

That he'd called out gave her even more hope that the note she carried was truthful. She'd have to pray hard and beg the archbishop for forgiveness for her actions over these past days. She'd told more falsehoods than she could count.

William took her hand and led her toward the main gated door. The fat man was there waiting. There were no jeers this time. She wondered if the silence was because they were in awe of William. His presence was powerful. He would be vexed, and she would let him have his say. If what she held in her pocket had any value, that would surely temper his mood.

Once outside of the prison area and into the garden separating the structure from the great hall, William turned to her and held her by her shoulders. "If you ever pull an act like that again, I will build you your own prison. What were you thinking?"

"I was protecting my family, as you have been without my consult."

"There are so many ways this could have gone wrong."

"Aye, and so many ways this can go right. I have a letter from him in my pocket."

William's eyes grew wide. "What does it say?"

"I have not read it as I had to maintain my deception. We must bring it to the king and read it together."

That seemed to appease him somewhat, for he squeezed her shoulders and kissed the top of her head.

Agnes drew a deep breath to steady herself. Inside the king's solar the queen took her hands and led her to a thick, padded bench and passed her a goblet of something warm.

"Drink this," she said. "'Twill steady your nerves."

William sat beside her and placed his arm around her shoulder. "Do you need a few minutes?" he asked.

She was grateful he did not try to take her experience and inform the king without her involvement. Somewhere along the way, he'd understood that she had a voice as well.

"Nay. I am well enough to inform Your Majesty that I have a letter here written by my uncle." She reached in her pocket and withdrew the parchment.

"Well, Lady Montrose," the king said. "Read it out."

Agnes stood before them all and read.

"The letter reads, *I confess your letter surprises me, for you did not appear to be interested in my stories on our journey to Stirling. But yet here you are reciting those words precious to me and our brethren. You will find aid with them if you choose. But I will not give them up so easily. You must convince the king to release me. I will find you and bring you with me to somewhere safe. I know they won't let you see me again, so you can slip your notes to the servant named Archie. He is sympathetic to our cause and will ensure I receive them safely."*

Agnes looked at the king. "Archie?"

"Is loyal to me and has been warming up to John since he was imprisoned. We have been gleaning our own intelligence that way."

The king paced and stroked his beard. "What to do," he said.

"I know what we are not doing," William said as he stood. "We are not allowing my wife to be placed in harm's way one second longer. This business was folly from the start, and she will not be involved any longer."

"You do not get to make that decision, husband," Agnes said. "I will continue to assist His Majesty. In any way he deems necessary."

William scowled at her. They would argue this out, of that she had no doubt, but she would not do it in front of the king and queen.

"Now if it is all well with you, I should like to avail of a bath to wash away the stench of that place."

It would appear she would remain at Stirling Castle for the day at least. The king drew William into a conversation about the letter after Agnes passed it to him. The queen called for servants to attend Agnes and she was brought to her chamber. Not long after, as she sat in the tub with the hot water soothing her, she heard the door open and close softly. She'd sent away the servants, wanting only solitude. She didn't have to turn her head to know who'd entered the chamber.

Let the battle begin.

WILLIAM PULLED A chair over to the tub to sit by his wife. He reached out to brush a stray strand of hair off her shoulder and to the back of the tub. For a few moments he sat there brushing his fingers over the soft skin of her arm, staring into her eyes. His very existence was tied to her now. What happened to her happened to him as well, and nothing in this world could change that. His anger had stemmed from fear, but how could he express that in such a way that would not offend her?

"You are troubled by my participation in this business," she said after a time.

"I am," he said, not knowing how to best acknowledge his fears.

"Do you know what it was like to watch you almost die?"

Her words cut deep. He had not considered that side of it. It was his job to protect her, not the other way around.

"Then tell me," he said.

"I watched the life force all but drain from your body. Were it not for your healer's quick action, you would not be here right now."

"I am sorry you had to witness that," he said.

Agnes sat up and took his face into her hands. She gazed at him intently. "I could not sit around for the next attack. Do you understand that?"

"I do."

"But you are still vexed."

He took her hands in his and kissed them. It wasn't easy to be vulnerable with another person, to reveal his darkest fears.

"I was so afraid when I woke to find you gone. I would move mountains to protect you."

"William, I understand that fear. I felt it firsthand as I tended you. I was not convinced you would pull through the poison let alone the wounds. I simply had to try. Do you not see that?"

"Aye, I do, and I believe your actions may have helped. We can be strategic now in the missives we send him. I believe you should correspond with him, but you will not leave this place with him. You see that."

"I do. I have no intention of going with him, but I still think he will reveal something that will give their hideout away."

She stroked his face. "You look exhausted."

"I am, and I had hoped my wife would take an afternoon respite with me. The king offered for us to take our evening meal here, so we need not be seen any further this day."

William helped her out of the tub and into her shift. He pulled back the covers and stripped off his clothes to curl up with her. His body had not fully recovered and he was weak, but one word from her and he would use up every last ounce of strength to please her.

"I just want to lie like this," she said.

He smiled into her hair as he pulled her body to his and wrapped his arms around her. He tucked his knees into the backs of hers so that every part of her body touched his.

"I could stay like this forever," she whispered.

Aye, he agreed with her on that much. There were so many ways this business with her uncle could go wrong. They would be strategic, and she would have to write the letters, for he now knew her hand. He put thoughts of her uncle from his mind.

She was safe, he was safe, and the monarchs were safe. For now, that was all he could focus on. William raised a hand to stroke her hair and kissed the back of her head again. As if she needed another trait to endear her to him, she'd displayed bravery that was unexpected and awe inspiring. He had never known any woman, let alone a lady, who would put themselves into such potential peril. Agnes had. And she didn't excuse herself for it. She'd do it again. So he had to ensure speaking between them was open and clear. He would share everything with her concerning Mugdock and the village.

Never had he thought he would be married to a woman with whom he could share so much. The thought did not distress him; it was pleasing to him to have such a strong woman by his side. She truly had a soul that was one of a kind. Neville had told him he'd given her trews and a tunic to wear to conceal her at least a little as they rode to Stirling. He would have liked to have seen that.

The sun was high in the sky, but William's body felt like it was much later. Only when her breathing leveled out and he was sure she slept did he close his eyes and let sleep overtake him.

He woke sometime later to a dark chamber. He got out of bed and dressed then checked outside to see if a servant was close by. Fin was just coming down the hallway, so William stepped outside.

"How do you fare?" he asked. "Are you ready for your evening meal to be brought up?"

"I am well. Aye, and a fire stoked too, Fin. Thank you."

He returned to the chamber to find Agnes still sleeping so he lit all the candles he could find and arranged the table and chairs so they could sit by the fire. He would enjoy her company and the quiet this evening. A calm before the coming storm as it were.

They played with fire in facing this head on. Was it the right approach? Who knew? But they were in it now and there was no going back. Her father had washed his hands of sussing out the rebels, and her actions meant they had only one path forward.

Fin returned and upon William's urging was as quiet as a mouse as he ushered the servant and the kitchen maids to lay out a generous meal. Once everything was in its place, he motioned for Fin to join him outside.

Closing the door softly, he asked, "What do we really know about Archie?"

An odd look crossed Fin's face and one brow shot up quickly and he then masked his reaction. "He can be trusted, my lord, if that is what has you concerned."

"Aye. I see that the king does, and I now believe you do. How capable is he with this deception?"

"Far better than I would be," Fin said. "I'm told that I do not possess an ability to hide what I'm feeling."

William could see that. Still, he had to be sure. "How long have you known him?"

Fin smiled and William had an inkling of just how well the two knew each other.

"He started here five years ago. He has remained perfectly

loyal and was honored when the king asked for this special privilege."

William did not want to pry any longer. Fin shifted slightly and clasped his hands together. William hadn't meant to pry into anything personal, yet he still was not completely convinced of this man's ability to be adept at deception.

"It would appear, my lord, that Archie and Lady Montrose possess an ability you and I do not. I know you to be straightforward and honest. It takes a clever sort of mind to successfully convince others of their duality."

His words were true. William spoke from the heart and did not like deception, so he didn't employ it. If the king and Fin were so convinced, he would have to accept that and turn his focus to the next stage in this plot.

"Thank you, Fin. That is all we shall require this evening. Tell your Archie I thank him for his service to his king and to my family as well. You both will be rewarded greatly."

Fin placed his hand on his heart and bowed then retreated down the hallway.

William entered the chamber to find his wife seated at the table eyeing the delicious offering. She looked radiant in her linen shift and her dark hair unencumbered by a cap or pinned up. She was an ethereal creature, and he was captivated by her. That was all he had to worry about this night. The rest could wait until the morrow.

CHAPTER EIGHTEEN

D AYS PASSED AND the missives flowed back and forth between Agnes and her uncle with no new intelligence any of them could glean. Finally, the king crafted the last missive to indicate John would be moved to Edinburgh dungeon for his own protection as, falsely of course, other prisoners had caught wind of him and had made threats.

The king admitting he could not vouch for the safety of a prisoner under his own roof was a bit ridiculous, but they were desperate. The only way to ferret out the nest was to allow for his escape and track him. The whole plot didn't sit well with Agnes, and she'd voiced her concerns. Now sitting atop his horse with her husband and approaching Mugdock Castle, she could not shake the eerie sensation that they had missed something quite significant.

As they passed through the gates and the doors were closed and secured behind them, Agnes's senses went into high alert. Something was very off. William must have sensed it too for when he dismounted, he hesitated before reaching for her.

"William, what is it?"

"I'm not certain," he said almost to himself.

He took her hand once she was on the ground and walked slightly ahead of her toward the great hall. Inside he stopped, his body rigid for a moment, then relaxed. He reached for her hand

and tucked it inside his arm in a formal manner, then led her forward. Once Agnes was alongside William, she could see fully inside the hall. A woman and man whom she'd never met sat at the long table with the dowager countess seated at the head and the boys on the other side.

"Brother," the female said as she pushed back her chair and made her way toward them. The man beside her did the same. "They told me you'd nearly met your death and now I see you, I can believe it."

The woman's features were delicate, and her eyes were the same honey color as her brother. She did not wear the same kind and gentle way about her as her mother. Rather, Agnes sensed there was something under the surface she could not quite decipher. The woman cast her gaze slowly down Agnes's body and then up again to meet her eyes. Her lips were pursed in a straight line as if mirth never rested there.

"And so you came all this way to see that I was well with your own eyes. Truly, sister, I didn't know you cared for my wellbeing so keenly."

Keeping her eyes on Agnes, she said, "You are my eldest brother, are you not? If something were to happen to you, who would see to mother and the boys?"

"You've gone maternal too now, have you?" To the man, he said, "Seems like you have mellowed my sister, Connor. How on earth did you do that?"

Agnes had a sense that there had been some tension between them. This exchange certainly supported that notion. William had gone to great measures to ensure the security of the castle and everyone in it. And considering the threat, why would his sister take the risk of putting herself and her husband into the thick of it?

"My wife has a mind of her own, my lord, as you very well know."

From the corner of her eye, Agnes could see the man's fist clench and unclench. Hair raised like gooseflesh on her arms.

"Very well, then. Sister, Connor, may I introduce my wife, Lady Graham, Countess of Montrose. Agnes, this is my sister Elspeth and her husband Connor Munroe."

Never breaking her gaze, Elspeth curtseyed to Agnes and held out her hand. She touched cold fingers for a moment then let go. There was something unsettling about the woman far surpassing the stories told to her by the maids upon her first arrival at Mugdock.

"It is a pleasure to finally meet the woman who was able to tempt my brother to the altar. So many have tried before you, Lady Graham. Tell me, how was it you were able to make that happen?"

"Now, now, sister. There is no need to play tactics with your new sister. She will think you do not like her."

"Oh, on the contrary, brother. I believe she is the picture of perfection."

By this time his mother approached and urged them all to sit and feast. Agnes picked at the food but had somehow lost interest in her trencher. Each time she glanced their way, Elspeth's attention was focused in her direction.

When the meal was finished, Agnes made an excuse of a headache and made to return to her chamber. William kissed her forehead and as she turned to leave the hall, Elspeth called to her.

"I do hope you feel better, sister. I hope we can sit together this afternoon to get to know one another better."

Agnes nodded and left the hall. She swiftly made her way to her chamber and once inside with the door closed, expelled a deep breath. She was not a seer, and not the most astute judge of character, but something was not right.

She lay on the bed and pulled the coverlet over her. The past few weeks had been a whirlwind of activity between her marriage, blossoming love for William, and the dangerous encounter with her uncle and his journey to Edinburgh Castle so that he could escape. Surely, she was exhausted and that was why she felt unsettled by the unexpected company. That was all.

Elspeth was William's sister after all, and she deserved the respect that required. Agnes would take some time to rest and then she would seek out her new sister and give the woman a chance rather than make false assumptions with no evidence. She was better than that.

Long shadows crossed the floor when she woke sometime later that afternoon. A basin had been set out and some fresh cloths. Agnes dipped the cloth into the water and pressed it to her neck and forehead. Her slumber had aided her in energy, but she still had an overall odd sensation about her head, as though she were in a fog that wouldn't lift.

The evening meal would be soon, so she rummaged through her wardrobe to find a gown fitting for the occasion. The overly decorative ones from the queen were a bit much and hers from home were not quite appropriate in this heat. She thought about the other gowns that had been commissioned for her by her uncle and for the first time examined them.

Knowing what she did now, it was clear he was sending a message, for each gown somehow represented an aspect of the clans she could see were part of the rebel brethren. Och, aye, they were all there! Ross, Munroe, Sutherland, and MacKay, all represented by clan color and crest stitched into the sash on each gown. Had he intended to parade her around representing all those clans each night as a warning to the king? The whole business was wrought with twists and turns. For the first time she believed her uncle when he implied the web they'd weaved was cast wide with many connections. Perhaps too many for any of them to ever untangle.

She had to settle on a gown and so in a measure of good faith, she chose the one that had previously belonged to Elspeth. The gown was lovely and fit her well and she hoped her new sister would take it as a compliment. Agnes was not interested in there being any form of illustration of rank when the family was the only company and so this was the best choice. She was sure of it.

A knock sounded at the door and the maids entered. They

glanced at one another with their brows raised when they spied the gown Agnes had chosen.

"M'lady, are you *sure* that is the gown you wish to wear for the evening meal?"

"Is there any reason I should not wear it?" she asked. They both paused. Agnes would not condone their continued gossip about William's sister. When they didn't respond, she said, "Good. Then that is the gown I shall wear this evening and as a reward for your good sense, I will let you do whatever you wish to my hair."

That appeared to be enough for them to recover from their earlier hesitation. The maids set about to fuss over whether Agnes's hair should be up or down; covered or not. In the end they pinned her dark curls around her face and swept the rest back into a thick roll they covered with a mesh cap lined with gold stitching and dozens of pearls. They chose pearl earrings and a pearl necklace for her as well.

Agnes was pleased with the final look. She carried the air of a countess but was not so lofty as to hit anyone over the head with the knowledge. She hadn't seen William all afternoon and so assumed he'd been busy with estate business and catching up with his sister. Agnes left the chamber in search of them. She hoped the evening would prove pleasing for them all.

WILLIAM SAT BY the hearth lost in thought. While he loved his sister, having her here now with such turmoil about was not ideal. She had fallen hard for Connor. As a Munroe, he came from a strong family, though William did not know them well. As nephew to the chieftain, and with a good reputation, it was an easy match to make. He owned his own lands and kept company in good circles and so William erred on the side of Elspeth's preference. Lord knows she'd have put up the place had he refused. She'd kicked up enough noise each time he tried to find a suitable match for her.

He hadn't seen her since the wedding some months back and truth be told, had not even received a letter from her. But to show up unannounced because he'd been injured? Well, that was more emotion than he'd expect from her.

He shrugged it off and smiled when he spied his wife entering the hall for the evening meal. He was pleased she spent the afternoon resting after the days and weeks they'd endured. Her strength seemed to multiply by the day and he couldn't be prouder.

She was radiant as usual and wearing the gown he'd gifted her from his sister. Something told him Elspeth would either be quite flattered or vexed, and he suspected the latter. The woman was not one to be outshone and anyone who viewed Agnes in this gown would swear it had been made for her and not another woman.

"You are enchanting as always, my lovely wife." He leaned down and brushed his lips across hers.

"Aye, as are you," she said looking around. "Are we early?"

William offered the crook of his arm and when she slipped her hand through, he placed his atop. "I believe there shall only be us and my mother for supper this evening. Elspeth and Connor took the horses a while ago and said something about going into town."

Even as he said the words, they sounded odd. He'd never been overly concerned about Elspeth's whereabouts as long as she had a chaperone, which was usually their mother. He hadn't given much thought to her comings and goings as he was certain it centered around gowns and hats and ribbons and baubles. None of which interested him.

"But it will be dark soon," Agnes said. "Are we sure it is safe considering the threat?"

"Neville went with them and we are heavily guarded from here to there now and within the village. One would find it difficult to turn around without spying a guard."

Agnes shook her head. "I understand, but if you and I are targets, did that not extend to them?"

"They did not appear concerned earlier," he said, something tugging at the back of his mind.

He put it aside and focused on his lovely wife. They would share a quiet meal this eve with his mother, and he had to admit, that prospect was most welcome considering the events of late.

"There you are, my dears," his mother said. "I thought we would be a party of five this evening but have just learned Elspeth and Connor have made for some entertainment in the village."

His mother couldn't hide her expression well. She was disappointed as any mother would be when a child has left home and returned for a visit regardless of the circumstance.

"I must admit," William said as he pushed in Agnes's chair and then his mother's before taking his own, "I was quite surprised to see her. What was her expression as she left after her wedding?"

"It will be some years before I return," her mother said quietly.

Those words had cut his mother more than him.

"But I am pleased to see her now and such a confident woman she's grown into."

William exchanged a glance with Agnes who watched his mother with her brows drawn together. Did she sense something was off as well? He would be sure to probe her about it later. For now, he would enjoy the quiet meal and accept a peaceful respite.

It didn't last long.

Shouts from outside drew their attention to the entrance of the hall. He jumped to his feet and with one backward glance said, "Stay here," to his mother and wife.

Before he could reach the door, Elspeth and Connor burst through, clearly full of drink and stumbling around singing some sort of what he supposed was to be a melody. They both held bottles in their hands from which they drank heavily then proceeded to try another tune, apparently unaware there was anyone else in the hall.

"Elspeth!" he shouted.

They both stopped and looked at him then burst into laughter. By God, this was ridiculous. She was the sister of an earl, not some scullery maid cavorting about the country.

He grabbed her shoulders and shook. "Elspeth. What the hell do you think you're doing?"

She stopped then and swatted his hands away. "I'm doing whatever the hell I want," she said and took another long swig from the bottle.

William grabbed it from her and then Connor grabbed it back. "Do not touch my wife or her bottle," he said and handed it back to her.

"What is wrong with you two? I told you we have had a threat here and that we are trying to remain vigilant until this business is resolved."

They exchanged a glance and then burst into gales of laughter again.

William scratched his head and turned around to see what his mother and wife thought. He shrugged his shoulders. "Any ideas?"

When he turned back the two were staring at him hard. All mirth left the hall, and he had the foreboding sense the roof was about to blow off the place.

"I have an idea, brother," Elspeth said. "Why don't you hand over that wife of yours and maybe we will leave the family and the castle intact."

Her words took a while to sink in. When he looked at Connor it was to find him staring hard at Agnes and slicing his finger across his throat.

"Elspeth, you had better explain yourself and now, before I have you both run through."

"Well, I thought she was rather obvious," John Sinclair said stepping through the door and into full view. Near the door, he closed it and slid the bolt into place locking them in. How long had he been in the hall?

Behind him, Agnes shrieked as his mother whispered, "Who is he?"

"How did you get in here?" William said as he drew the dagger he kept at his side always.

"Are you really that daft, brother? Do you not think I know every nook and cranny of this place and of the many holes you left in your formidable security detail."

"So what now?" William asked. "Do you really think the three of you can best me to get to Agnes."

"No. We don't," John said. "And we don't have to. If she wants to see her parents again, she will come willingly, otherwise they will be dead before daybreak." To Agnes, he said. "And you. You lying bitch. I will have my vengeance upon you. To think you could outwit we who have been plotting for years. You think you can outsmart and unravel a network that goes beyond a handful of rebels. You poor little daft wench. Never fear, niece. Your precious queen will get what's coming to her too."

To his horror, Elspeth grinned and nodded her head. He looked at the three and the threat they posed. He glanced at the door. Where the hell were the king's guard.

"Oh, you wonder where your protectors are?" John asked. "They're with everyone else trying to put out the fires that somehow lit the town ablaze this afternoon. Tsk, tsk, tsk, Montrose. You really should take better care of your people."

William's rage surfaced in that moment as he lunged for John. He almost caught him when something stung his back. He knew in an instant what it was as he dropped to the floor. The last thing he heard before passing out was his wife screaming his name and his sister's maniacal laughter. He prayed to God and all that was holy he would not die this night. For their sake perhaps he should because if he didn't he would hunt down and draw and quarter each and every one of them.

CHAPTER NINETEEN

S HE DID NOT possess the strength to lose him a second time. Where she found the courage, Agnes did not know. In the next moment, she too lunged forward toward Elspeth, grabbed hold of her shoulders while kicking her legs out from beneath her. With William's mother shrieking in the background, Connor tying William's hands behind his back, and she sitting atop Elspeth and holding onto her hands, the scene must have looked quite horrific to anyone who might happen upon them.

Hands dug into Agnes's hair as she was yanked off Elspeth and flung her aside to hit the wall. She'd gotten her hands out in front of her in time to protect herself from receiving a nasty blow to the head.

"You filthy bitch!" Elspeth leapt at her but was caught by John and restrained.

"She is no good to us maimed. You must remember the plan."

Elspeth immediately backed off. Whatever hold John held over her must be great for she appeared to revere him as though he were her superior.

His words sent shivers down Agnes's spine. This business was far from over and for the first time she believed all would not be well. She had so many questions and without William now to protect her, she considered she might never find the answers.

"Get up," John said as he kept Elspeth at bay who looked like she wanted to tear Agnes apart one limb at a time.

"Why?" she asked.

"Because if you don't," John said, "you will regret it. And believe me when I say, niece, you will also soon regret your attempt to deceive me. Though your fickle plot was enough to help me escape, it was not enough for me to give up the location of our band."

He reached down and lifted her up by the shoulder. "Now be a good lass and keep your mouth shut," he said as he turned to Elspeth.

"This way," she said and moved to the back of the hall to the side of the hearth. "Quick, behind here," she said leading to a narrow passageway Agnes didn't know existed.

"Where are you taking me?" she asked. Hair prickled at her nape and uneasiness swept over her as she realized they had left William hogtied and his mother shrieking while Connor tied her to a chair.

John shoved her forward as the first pounding began at the hall door on the other end. Someone must have realized finally the danger that had set up on them.

"Will they find us in here?" he asked Elspeth.

"It is not likely. These passageways have not been used in years, and at this point only William and my mother would know about them."

"Where do they lead?"

"They will bring us outside of the castle walls. But we must be careful. Once the guards are inside, they will seek an alternative exit and since Connor is administering more of the poison to my mother at this moment, it is unlikely she or William will wake for many hours."

Agnes tried hard to keep her wits about her. The last comment gave her some relief in that at least they weren't planning to kill them, rather render them helpless until they could make their escape. The pathway was dark and the sound of Elspeth feeling her way along was unnerving.

"What do you plan to do with me?" she asked.

"If it were up to me, you'd already be dead," Elspeth said with such a matter-of-fact tone Agnes didn't doubt it for a second.

That she might live was likely due to her uncle; the irony was not lost on her. William would be beside himself when he woke to find her missing again. But this time was far worse than the last.

"Enough, Elspeth. Less talking and more movement. I won't rest until we are away from this damned place and somewhere safe."

She'd keep that nugget to herself as well. If she could find a way to delay them, she might yet survive this ordeal.

"Why won't you tell me what you plan to do with me?" she asked him.

"You'll find out soon enough," he said.

If his intent was to ensure she remained on edge and terrified, he was achieving his goal. Agnes's guts were coiled as tight as could be. Her blood pounded in her ears, and she was sure much more of this and she would surely retch. Some part of her was convinced her own uncle would not see harm come to her. On the other hand, he was scheming enough and dedicated enough to this plan to outsmart the king's own guardsmen and walk straight into the castle and snatch her away. She would of course give credit to William who would have never suspected his sister's involvement in this rebellion.

By God, when her uncle had said they were spread far and wide, he hadn't exaggerated. If an earl's own sister could be involved, there was no limit to the levels to which this cause had reached. And that was it. Everyone had sold them short, especially William. Her heart ached at how he would feel when he woke.

In the distance she could hear shouting and the sound gave her hope. She had to think fast if she were to find any way to delay them exiting the castle. The hallway was rather narrow with lots of twists and turns. She could try to trip, but then John would likely just pick her up and carry her. Still, it would slow his movements. She didn't want to really hurt herself in case she needed all her parts in good working order should she need it.

"We turn here," Elspeth said as they approached a split in the passageway.

Agnes turned to see if she could make out anything down the other passageway, but John urged her forward before she could really glean what might be there and if it might offer some security should she find a way to escape.

After several minutes the passageway widened and light from somewhere ahead brightened their way enough so Agnes could detect a doorway down at the end. The shouting she heard earlier was now completely gone; her uneasiness returned with a vengeance.

"How will we know if he made it out?" John asked.

It was then Agnes realized Connor had not followed them. If he hadn't gone through the main door, and hadn't followed them, did that mean there was another way out still?

"We will know shortly," she said as she pressed her ear to the door.

Agnes was out of time. She could kick herself now for not fake tripping over something earlier. Dammit! She had to do something before they left the castle or who knows when she might have another chance. At the very least she would have to leave a sign somehow to let William know where she was.

Reaching into her pocket she searched until she found only one item. She balled up the handkerchief and pulled her hand from her pocket. Squeezing the fabric tight, she willed it to land somewhere William might find it.

Elspeth turned back to them with a smile on her face. "He's there."

She opened the door wide and as John pushed her through, she tossed the handkerchief behind him hoping it landed in a good place.

"Through here," Elspeth said as she led the party through a small opening in the garden.

The time was upon her. She must do something now or she might never find another chance.

Agnes opened her mouth and drew in a deep breath. John clamped his hand across her mouth as if foreseeing she might do something like that. The only thing she could do now was to break free from him. She bucked and kicked at him and tried to squirm out of the hold he had on her, but it was no use. He was too strong.

"We can't travel with her like this. We can't trust her," Connor said. "Here, let me hit her over the head with this rock."

"You'll kill her and she'll be of no use to us then," John said.

"Here," Elspeth said as she withdrew a vial from her pocket together with a piece of cloth. She poured the liquid on the cloth and returned the vial to her pocket. "We will have to be quick," she said to John.

As soon as John's hand lifted from her mouth, Agnes let out as much sound as she could before it was covered again by the cloth. Pressed against her nose and mouth, she had no choice but to inhale and as soon as she did her mind turned to fog and her limbs grew heavy. She didn't fear for her life, but she did fear that asleep she would have no way to leave any further clues for William to find her. Her last waking thought was of him and how she had failed him—failed them all.

WHEN HE WOKE, William found himself half sitting against the stone wall. A cloth was placed on his head and Old Nan sat beside him. His mother rested, her head in her hands, and wept at the table. He looked around for Agnes, somehow knowing she was not there. Dozens of guards and clansmen all spoke at once making the dull ache in his head worse.

"I have to admit, laddie, I'm not fond of finding you like this," Old Nan said. When he made to get up, she placed a surprisingly strong hand on his shoulder. "Not yet. Twice poisoned in a short time and the only thing that saved you this time was the size of you and a smaller quantity."

He understood her words, but they needed to act, and fast. The more time that passed, the less likely he would find Agnes before they secured her some place she might never be discovered.

"You're awake," Neville, his steward said. "How do you fare?"

"I am well enough. What do we know?"

"We managed to save most of the village. Only two homes burned and none of the merchant structures; both the forge and the tannery are intact."

That was good news. He'd provide materials and have those homes rebuilt immediately. He would not have a family displaced for any longer than necessary and he'd put them up in the inn in the meantime.

"And Agnes?"

"We know they used the old passageways, but beyond that…"

"Do we know which one they used?"

Neville pulled something from inside his tunic and handed it to William. His whole world spun around him as his heart squeezed tight. She'd left a breadcrumb and by God he would tear the country apart to find her. Ignoring Old Nan's advice, William managed to stand. He vowed he'd never find himself in this state again.

"How long has it been since they took her?"

"By our estimation, at least an hour. It appears they only poisoned you both enough so they could make their escape."

"William, I am so sorry," his mother said from the table. Her eyes were red and puffy. "I should have seen to her more after your father passed. Should have guided her more."

William placed his hand on her shoulder. "I don't believe anything could have been done for her part. There's always been something off about Elspeth; you know that. And now we know all those years she blamed the boys for her doing, a seed of evil had firmly rooted within her heart. It appears that root has found firm soil in which to thrive. She will be stripped of any funding from this day forward and will never be permitted entry to these lands again. Does everyone hear me?"

He turned to Neville, whose face was flushed. William wouldn't take his annoyance out on anyone in particular, but he had considered safety and security at great length and even he'd been blindsided by his sister's involvement. Aye, it was true a stranger would have never gotten through the gates, but a family member who'd never been suspected was a sideways betrayal he could have never anticipated. Brilliant. But completely unpredictable.

"The right or left passage?"

"Left," Neville said. "So you know where that leads."

"Aye, I do. Have you sent men to intercept?"

"I have."

"Chances?"

Neville shook his head.

"Neville, I must know what you think as I do not have all the pieces to do so myself."

Neville shuffled on his feet and cast his gaze downward. Reaching around to scratch the back of his neck, he said, "I don't think the chances are good that we will find her this night."

William placed his hands on the table. How he longed to place his head in his hands and give in to the ache in his heart like his mother. But he didn't have that luxury.

Standing, he motioned for the guards by the door to come closer. "You four will ride hard to Stirling Castle and inform the king of what has transpired here including the fires at the village and the abduction of my wife. The king will secure his own household, but you can tell him, I will accept nothing less than a complete and thorough search of every dwelling between here and Munroe lands. They are now considered enemies of the crown in my eyes, and I suspect will be through the king's as well."

When the men left, he turned back to Neville. "My mother and brothers are to be confined to their chambers until I return. See to it food and drink are brought up at the appropriate mealtimes and that they are placed in the adjoining chambers with guards posted outside the doors."

Thankfully his mother didn't protest, though he suspected his younger brothers would. Hopefully it wouldn't be for long and though they'd clearly got what they came for, he couldn't be sure if there was a further agenda against his family now considering the source. At least he could do one small thing by cutting off her money. He'd thought it strange at the time when she asked for her dowry in increments rather than upfront as was customed. He now realized that his father would think the first large sum was it, so they could then use the remaining increments to fund this rebellion. Well, no more.

The only piece of comfort was that maybe, just maybe the Munroe chief was not involved. Though his comments for the king's ears would suggest otherwise, the king would compare his own intelligence to the happenings here and come to the appropriate conclusion. Even if the chief was not involved, he would have to take responsibility for the actions of his clansmen. Arson and abduction of a countess were both punishable by death. He shook his head. Was his sister truly prepared for the consequences of her actions? Was the cause truly that important?

"Does that mean I am not to accompany you, my lord?"

Neville was his most trusted friend. They'd been through much together since his father's passing, but these two attacks had weakened the man somehow, and William needed time for his faith in him to return. For now, and with such heavy security about, here was the best place for him.

"Aye, you will remain here and ensure the continued security of my family."

The man bent his head low which tugged on William's affection, but he could not and would not take further chances with this business. If the man's feelings were hurt, William couldn't help that. Did he blame him? No. But at the moment, he was compromised.

William then turned to his mother. "You will accompany Neville to your chamber now, Mother. See to it you stay there and keep the boys in the room adjoining yours."

Used as a nursery many years ago, there was still one bed and another that could be brought over from one of the other rooms so both boys could sleep in comfort. They'd be bored, aye, and his mother would be contrary about being restricted from the garden, but he would not bend in this regard until all of this business was over once and for all.

William spoke then with the guards he selected to accompany him on his own search. There were only a few places they could get to in the dark from that passageway, so he wanted to waste no more time before the path grew cold.

With six guards, they mounted their horses and moved around to the back of the castle to where the pathway led to a small opening in the brush. These passageways had been built early in the castle's history as a way for the family to escape should they come under siege. They'd not been used in years, by William's estimation, certainly not since the curtain wall and guard tower had been put in place. He hadn't considered them at all when ensuring the security of the perimeter initially. Why would he? Save for Neville, the family were the only ones who knew they were there. When this was all over, he'd see to it they were sealed shut for good.

Christ's teeth, how had his world become so turned upside down? One minute he was reveling in the newfound joy he'd discovered with Agnes. Now he was tracking in the dark to hopefully find some clue as to which direction they might have traveled once they hit the road. At that point, he'd have to make a leap of faith, and he prayed to God to steer him in the right direction.

CHAPTER TWENTY

WHEN AGNES WOKE, all was dark around her save for a soft glow from a fire across from where she lay. She tried not to make much motion to alert anyone that she was awake so she could glean as much information as possible. She couldn't be sure if they would drug her again, or worse, so she'd keep quiet and see what she could learn.

Long moments passed with no sound until muffled voices sounded from outside. Boots shuffled near her and a person she'd not realized sat right beside her stood and moved to the door. When it opened, a deep male voice said, "It's about time."

"Aye well, 'tis not so easy to see in the dark now, is it?"

She didn't recognize either of the two male voices, but she'd recognize the third anywhere.

"Has she awoken yet?" John asked.

"No, not yet, she's been snoring away. Now that's a sound I never thought I'd hear coming from a countess no less."

"Aye, and you'll not hear it again if you repeat it," John said. "She should be awake by now."

Agnes felt his hand on her shoulder as he shoved back and forth. Something told her to keep up her ruse for as long as she could.

"Give her fifteen more minutes, then put her in the cart anyway. We have to keep moving."

That might just be long enough for her to devise a way to leave another crumb for William. She prayed he'd seen the first and could determine something useful from it. Agnes took stock of what she could feel around her. She lay on some kind of cot with blankets beneath her. Even if she could move her hands to tear off a piece she would be heard. No, she needed to think of something else. Something he would recognize as hers.

When it came to her, she smiled to herself, careful not to make any facial movement.

After what was definitely not fifteen minutes, John said, "That's long enough. Snuff out that fire. I told you we shouldn't have lit it in the first place."

John approached and lifted her in his arms then carried her to the cart outside and placed her under a canvas. She'd been careful to have loosened her slipper so that when she was picked up, it would fall off naturally. The pride she had in herself in that moment would have to be cherished at another time. From one small hole in the canvas, she could see that John rode beside her. Releasing the other slipper onto the roadway would prove difficult, but she was determined to do so. And at some point, John would not believe she still slept, so she took in these moments to craft another move.

Not long after, the rough roadway offered that opportunity. The cart jolted from a deep hole in the road the driver would never have seen in the dark. Agnes sat upright and flicked off the canvas looking around wildly as if she'd only now just woken. She pushed back the canvas and made to climb over the side, dropping her slipper at the same time then pulling back inside the cart. She made sure their attention was focused on her and so kept her movements random.

"Where am I?" she asked in as much of a panicked voice as she could muster.

When the driver made to stop the cart, John said, "No, keep moving. I'll handle her."

The sound of a sword being unsheathed was unmistakable.

Agnes froze. Surely, he wouldn't. She felt a sting at her neck and a soft chuckle.

"I could end you here and now and you'd never be found. As tempting as that is, niece, I have other plans for you. This is your only warning. If you make any noise to draw attention to us, I will run this sword through your neck faster than you can say loyalty. Now lie down and pull that canvas over you. If you make so much as a movement, you'll never see your precious earl again."

Agnes did as she was told, uninterested in riling him further. She was grateful now for her earlier stealthiness. It wouldn't be long before he discovered her deception, and there was no telling what he would do.

Under the canvas and with only one peep hole, there was little Agnes could decipher regarding her surroundings. She focused her energy on thoughts of William. In her mind he was closing in on them and the next time the canvas was pulled back it would reveal him reaching for her. But he was not closing in on them and for the next few hours, she lay under fabric that smelled of rotten cabbage. The cart bounced and bucked so much she was sure she'd be full of bruises. She tried to keep her mind focused lest she fall into despair. One way or another she'd need her wits if she were to survive this ordeal.

Eventually the cart came to a halt and John pulled back the canvas. He gathered her up and plopped her on her feet then pushed her forward to another dwelling. The first streaks of gray crossed the sky, so she knew from that they'd been traveling all night. How many miles that might have been and how far behind was William she could not estimate.

Agnes tried not to wince from the sharp rocks digging into her feet as she walked forward, but when one particularly dug in, she couldn't help but let out a soft "ouch".

"What is this?" John asked in a sharp tone. He lifted her skirt and glared at her when he spied her stocking feet. "Where are your slippers?"

Agnes firmly planted her lips together and shook her head. When the back of his hand struck her face, she saw stars and crumpled to the ground. If there was any justice at all in this world, William would find the slippers and save her before her uncle could knock the life force from her. She did not consider herself capable of hating another human, but she was fast growing to despise this man.

"Do you honestly think dropping your precious slippers will help the earl find you?" He laughed in the most devilish way she'd ever heard in her life. The sound made her guts lurch and without warning she retched on the ground.

John lifted her by her arm just underneath her shoulder and shoved her forward to the cabin. When the door opened and Elspeth stood there wearing an evil grin, Agnes lost her guts again.

William, please find me before it's too late.

"Red looks good on you, sister," Elspeth said, taunting her. "But my dress does not."

Once inside the cabin with the door closed, Elspeth tore at the gown and by the time she was done, Agnes was covered in scratches with her arms wrapped around herself for modesty. Standing in a cold cabin with no heat and only in her shift, she trembled and shook.

"That's enough," John said. He snatched a quilt and threw it at Agnes.

She took it and scrambled away from them to wrap herself up. Sitting on another cold cot in another cold cabin she determined she would take no more risks.

"How much longer before he arrives?" Elspeth asked, glancing at Agnes then focusing her attention on John.

"He should be here soon. Then we can reach our safehouse at the Devil's Pulpit. No one in their right mind will think to look there. We can hold up for the time it takes to put the rest of our plan into action and this one," he said, pointing his thumb at Agnes, "will finally prove her worth. The king will not refuse our demands now if he wishes to save her hide."

Connor showed up then. "We are all set and should make haste. I've heard rumblings of a large search party."

John lifted Agnes again, blanket and all, into a much larger cart that had many boxes and barrels. She assumed those were supplies. She had to leave a sign, but how? She had no parchment, no more clothes left to offer, and though her tattered gown would leave them in no doubt she'd been there, how could she signify where they were going?

Agnes gripped her quilt tighter. Despair washed over her. She might have some value now, but it was clear based on her treatment up until now, once they achieved their goal, she would have no more value and she would be killed. Of that, now she was completely certain. Her own uncle and William's sister placed no value on her life and would use it to seek riches or whatever it was this band of rebels wanted and then they would discard her as though she were the vermin of the world. A small tear trickled down her cheek. Agnes turned her head to the wall so no one would see.

WHEN WILLIAM LEARNED of what had been found in a cottage northwest of Mugdock, his heart soared. Now holding Agnes's slipper in his hands, he hoped against all hope she was unharmed. If they continued to travel this way, there were few options for them unless, again, they had unexpected supporters. On the trail just away from the cabin, William spied the second slipper. He dismounted and quickly retrieved it to compare it to the first. A perfect match. He looked at the road and could see thin grooves which could only come from a cart.

Mounting his horse, he tracked the grooves for miles until they led to a second cabin. In it the sight that met his eyes stopped him in his tracks. Scattered about the floor was the gown Agnes had been wearing when they'd taken her. By Christ, if there was one hair misplaced on her head, he'd throttle those responsible, sister or not.

William was ready to pound someone. Instead, he turned and slammed his hand hard against the cabin wall. When he did, a small piece of parchment fell from one of the beams above him. He opened it to find the words this band had continued to repeat to themselves and to each other. Seemingly unimportant, he shoved it in his pocket then paused and retrieved it to read again. The parchment was of good quality as was the ink, for there was no smudging. The writing was fine as though the person who wrote it had been properly taught.

Elspeth.

She'd been here before Agnes's abduction. Understanding this and thoughts of the peculiar dowry arrangement got him thinking. Just how long before their marriage had Elspeth been a part of these rebels and their cause? Something niggled at him. Some connection he'd yet to discern that was the key to this whole business where his family was concerned.

For now, he would continue to focus on finding Agnes, and after that he would not rest until he unraveled the entirety of the plot.

William mapped out each community between there in a northwestern direction. If their end was Munroe lands, he'd have thought they would head northeast.

But what was northwest? Some small communities across various clan boundaries, but nothing came to mind to convince him they had sought refuge with an ally. If not that, then what? Another hiding place? With half the king's guard tearing apart Scotland, William couldn't figure out where they'd be.

After two days of searching with little rest, he determined he needed to return to Mugdock to recharge and regroup. They could not possibly be in any sort of typical lodging. And if they were squirreled away in some cave somewhere, they might never be found.

With low spirits he returned to Mugdock. Neville met him in the hall for an update to which he confessed he had none.

"Your mother has been asking for you constantly."

"No doubt because the boys are testing her last nerve."

"No, I believe it may be far more serious than that."

William examined Neville for sincerity. The man looked as worn out as William felt. He'd dark circles under his eyes and his entire outward manner was unkempt which was grossly out of character.

"Do you know what it is about?"

"I do, but you cannot hear these words from me. This is for your mother to tell you and she alone."

William was tired and hungry, but he would see to his mother first and then to himself. There was nothing more he could do for Agnes in his current state.

He knocked softly on her chamber door then entered. She opened it immediately and then ushered him to the hearth and passed him a trencher of food and some ale.

"Have you discovered her yet?"

Taking a bite of bread and then a drink of ale, William shook his head. He placed the trencher and goblet aside. "Mother, Neville tells me you have something I need to hear. Do tell me now for I am travel weary and in need of rest so I can resume the search on the morrow."

He loved his mother dearly, but she'd changed since his father died. More often than not, she resorted to her own musings and could often be heard mumbling to herself.

"You are a good son. Loyal," she said.

The word perked his attention. Why would she choose that one considering everything happening at the moment.

"Mother, what is it you wish to tell me?"

His mother wrung her hands as she took the seat opposite him. Tears welled in her eyes then spilled over onto her cheeks.

"I never thought it would come to this."

"Mother, what are you talking about?"

"Elspeth. She adored your father. Believed every word he ever spoke and like your Agnes, loved to hear him tell stories."

William had never known his father by any other means than as a good kind man who worked hard for his family, their clan, and the crown.

"What stories?"

She drew in a deep breath. This was hard for her, whatever she had to confess, but he was more convinced by the moment it was significant.

"At first, they were mythical, about faeries and witches and ghosts. As your sister devoured them each night, your father became more comfortable in the telling. He loved every moment in delighting her and she became lost in them. I would hear her talking to herself about them and in some ways the stories overlapped. I was worried and voiced my concerns to your father. So he decided to change their topic. He told her of our histories, our clan, and of the king, and eventually the subject turned to the rebels. She was insatiable in her thirst for knowledge about them. She had to know why they believed in the old king and not the current."

William's guts lurched as he heard the words flow from his mother.

"He told her what he knew and which families were supporters and which were loyal to the crown. Then finally the dreaded question came."

He knew it before his mother even spoke. Everything clicked into place. All the rejections from suitors William tried to arrange for her. There was nothing wrong with the gentlemen. It was the families from which they hailed. She'd been bent on marrying a rebel all along.

"But surely Father explained their actions were treasonous. That these were not people with whom we associated."

His mother slumped in her chair and leaned her head back. Drawing another deep breath, she said, "Your father was so delighted in her interest, he embellished his acknowledgement of their cause. She seemed so very proud of him when he said he supported them, but could not tell another soul, not even you, lest he be discovered."

He couldn't believe his ears! How his own father could be so careless was unfathomable. But it all made sense. All the trouble Elspeth had caused.

"Surely Father could see in time the damage this falsehood had caused."

"By the time he did, it was too late. She would hear no opposition from him and then he passed, taking his shame with him."

And now she held his beloved Agnes captive, subjecting her to Christ only knew the level of torture. His need to find her increased tenfold. There would come a time when she would no longer be useful to them. And that only meant one thing. They would accept nothing less than the king off the throne, and once that happened, Agnes would serve no purpose.

Elspeth had to be behind much of this current plot. These rebels had been around for years with little damage ensuing save for a few riots here and there, but little harmed and nothing like this. Perhaps if she was the driving force, something else could be gleaned from the words she so cherished from their father.

"You must recount every story you are familiar with that father told Elspeth."

"But what good would that do?"

"I believe if she hung off his every word, as you say, that something in the execution of this plot might be buried in those stories. She used the secret passageways after all, and I recall the night father told both of us about them. I remember her now sitting on the edge of her chair and insisting we take a torch and explore them right then and there."

"You truly believe something in these stories might offer us a clue as to where she's taken Agnes?"

"Aye, Mother. I am as certain as you and I are sitting here. There's a clue in those stories. And now you must tell them to me. Leave out no detail."

William reached for the trencher and goblet and settled into his chair. He waited for his mother to begin and then he listened intently. He would ferret out this detail even if it took them all night.

Chapter Twenty-One

AGNES HAD NO idea how many days passed. She'd eaten so little and grew weaker by the moment. They offered her only some water, stale bread, and half-cooked potatoes, but she longed for a trencher of meat and cheese. Her mouth watered each time they ate, which seemed to know no limit by way of expense. Most days she huddled under her blanket with her back turned to them until Elspeth yanked off the blanket and shoved her toward the door to relieve herself. Twice a day she was allowed whether she needed to or not. And she was needing to less and less with such little sustenance.

They argued constantly about the path forward. The end goal, it appeared, was to unseat the king. Elspeth expressed more doubt as to how that would be possible as the days grew into a week, then two.

Outside this time, a wave of nausea overtook her. She retched until there was nothing left to come out of her. She had long given up trying to figure out where they'd taken her this time. Tall banks meant she couldn't escape that way, and a long stream with water that appeared to run red gave her chills each time she looked at it. Once she was sure she saw a dark figure atop a rock that resembled a pulpit like the priests used in church. Either way, the entire area held a strange, unsettling air.

"You've been doing that more and more," Elspeth said, drawing Agnes back to the present and as if attempting to display a wee smidge of empathy. "Perhaps I can get you some broth after we eat if there's anything left."

Agnes wasn't naive enough to think the woman would aid in her escape, but she might make a slip up and Agnes would quietly listen for it. "Thank you," Agnes whispered, hoping she would follow through, but not having any faith considering her treatment up to this point.

Back inside the cabin, John gave her an odd look then handed her a warm cup of mead. For a moment, Agnes stared at it not quite knowing if it was an offering in good faith or poison to be rid of her once and for all.

She reached for the cup enjoying the way the warmth spread from her hand to her arm. "What is it?"

"'Tis warm mead and nothing else. Drink it up and you might be offered more later on," he said then turned back to the fire.

Agnes brought the cup to her cot then covered herself as usual, sipping the sweet drink. The liquid did wonders to break the chill from her bones and settled her belly. She wondered what had brought about this sudden change in the both of them. To her knowledge, a new missive hadn't arrived in the past few days. They usually came every three days with news of the search and reward for Agnes and also the growing bounty on their heads. Were they in a small way trying to make amends? For what they'd already done to her or what they were about to do?

"We have no choice, you know," Elspeth said as she approached Agnes and offered her another blanket.

Agnes' confusion grew, as she worried more about the change in their bearing. They weren't fired up like they had been about their cause. Rather, they appeared more solemn as if they were about to make a choice that was not agreeable.

She kept her thoughts to herself for the remainder of the day. The mead had done its job and warmed her enough so that a little clarity emerged. She'd been concerned that the cramping in her belly and her tender breasts were because of the lack of nutrition, but now recognizing she'd not bled since her wedding night, she knew.

Her entire course of thought changed in that moment. She would find a way out of this if it was the last thing she did. And it wouldn't be. By the grace of God and her own will, she would save herself and her bairn. In her heart she knew she could. She just needed her wits about her now more than ever.

She watched as they packed up a few things, glancing her way from time to time until finally John stood before her. "You will be fine here for a few days," he said. "We will leave the food and drink and there's wood for a fire."

She couldn't believe her ears. "You—you're leaving me here?" Was she excited or terrified? Her mind flipped between the two, settling on the former. She would keep her hopes up that she could find something to put on the fire to make it smoke to help William find her.

"Where will you go?" she asked not expecting an answer.

John hesitated at the door and opened his mouth to say something then closed it and left the cabin. Elspeth glanced once at her before she too left the cabin. She then heard a sound that made her belly turn in knots. The determined click of a lock and then the tapering sound of a carriage moving off into the distance.

The first thing she did when there was no more sound from outside was to try the latch. She was firmly trapped inside the cabin. For the moment she was safe and had enough food and drink to keep her. She stoked the fire and went rummaging for something to make a stew. Once that was done, she searched for additional clothing, for she could not be sure who would find her, but she was certain someone would. In her heart she was absolutely positive.

She sang to herself and to her bairn as she organized her provisions and even found a small chamber pot that would only do for a day or two then she'd have to find an alternative.

Why they had up and left her after all this time, she could not say. Did their brethren forsake them? Had their hiding place been offered up to save someone else's neck? Agnes would have no way to know, but a reason like that seemed the most likely.

As she sat at the table on her first night alone, wearing a hunter's plaid she'd found hanging by the door, she tucked her feet under her and sipped at the stew she managed to pull together. Like the mead from earlier, it was a hug from the inside out. She cleaned out her bowl as best as she could and placed it near the hearth to dry. She wanted to ration everything including water so she would use the fire to clean the iron bowl and brush out the cinders that way.

Moving about the cabin, she organized the bedding and swept the floor, trying to keep herself busy lest she let her mind loose with horrific thoughts of what was to become of her. An image of the figure on the rock a ways up the stream flashed before her mind's eye. She pushed it away as hard as she could and instead conjured up some of her favorite stories from her childhood.

"Oh, Bregdi, if only you could come and save me now," she said out loud. A moment later a sound from outside made her freeze.

A low growl was followed by a deep rhythmic yowl that almost sounded like words. Agnes backed away from the cabin door as the creature scratched at it, hissing and making that horrifying yowling.

She hopped onto the bed and covered herself entirely with the blanket, leaving just enough of her exposed to peek out at the door. When she did, she noticed for the first time a small crack of light coming in through the bottom part of the door. The light was blocked and then she could see it again.

Curious, she leaned closer to the door just as a small paw poked in through the opening. The hissing continued as did the odd language it spoke. Agnes squinted her eyes as the paw came through for a second time. She pushed back the blankets and rested her head in her hands.

Surely nothing to be trifled with, but the realization that a

Highland wildcat was outside the door, rather than some evil spirit, comforted her.

Agnes rummaged through the basket of food and found what she sought. She placed a small piece of cheese near the crack in the door and waited. A heartbeat later the paw returned to claim the cheese. The sight warmed her heart. Perhaps Bregdi had sent protection for her after all. Or, at the very least, some company lest she go mad left with only her thoughts to see her through.

WITH ONLY ONE more location to explore, William's hope dwindled with each passing moment. He'd practically checked under every rock and in every crevasse he could find over past days, which now seemed to bleed into one another. He had no idea when he slept or ate last and was practically on his last legs. This final spot must be it.

The Devil's Pulpit was not easy to locate, and the descriptions were vague at best among those who lived close by. He suspected that had more to do with fear than anything else. If she was there, he'd find her, and if she wasn't, he was out of ideas.

William followed the stream until he came to the tall dark red embankments covered in foliage. The stream ran red, likely from the iron in the soil and surrounding cliffs, but he had to admit, it was an unnerving sight. According to the locals, the only place a lodging could be built was on the other side of the pulpit. He approached the rock formation with caution.

Just as he was almost upon it, a wildcat jumped up onto the rock and stared hard at him. It yowled and mouthed some kind of cat gibberish that made the hair stand on the back of his neck. The cat meowed loudly and then jumped off the rock and ran on ahead of him. It looked back several times and then ran forward again. Did it want him to follow?

Having no other ideas, William followed the wildcat up the

stream to where the tall embankments evened off and the land leveled. He smelled the smoke before he saw it. When he turned the corner and the cabin came into view, he dismounted and followed the cat to the door.

The cat meowed loudly again.

Shuffling came from within the cabin and a soft voice called, "Here kitty, kitty. I have more cheese for you."

"Agnes?"

"William?"

"Aye, 'tis me!"

"William, I'm locked in. Can you get me out of here?"

William's heart was in his throat. The cat stepped casually to the side as if knowing what would happen next.

"Stand away from the door," he shouted.

He heard stumbling from inside. "I'm away," she called.

William lunged for the door and hit it with his shoulder with all his might. Pain exploded down his arm from his previous injury, but he ignored it when the door gave way and he fell to the cabin floor.

Agnes was on him in an instant. The smell of the place was enough to make any strong stomach heave. He gathered her up and brought her outside, sitting with her near the stream. William wrapped his arms around her and rocked her. Tears streamed down his face, and he looked upward and silently thanked God for leading him to her. In that moment the cat approached them.

She held out her hand and the cat sniffed then licked it, brushed up against them, and then took off down the trail and out of sight.

"His job is done," she said quietly, leaning her head against his chest.

"How long where you in there alone?"

"I scratched a line for each night, and I think there are five."

William leaned back to look at her face. She was in desperate need of a wash and some clean clothes.

"Did you have any food?"

"Aye, they left me enough for about a week so I would have been good for a couple more days. But I had nowhere to empty my—"

"You don't need to worry about any of that. Come, let's get you somewhere safe," he said as he wrapped his cloak around her and lifted her atop his horse. Once he mounted, he shifted her so that she was practically in his lap. She was quiet and he was satisfied with that. She'd been through an incredible ordeal and would need time to process it all. As would he.

He rode as hard and as fast as he could with her toward the nearest town. He'd been staying at a small inn and knew the owner would be discreet in the manner in which Agnes was found. By God, he'd found her. Neither John, his sister, nor any other power in this world would keep him from administering justice upon them.

He'd heard that one by one, the rebels had backed away which must have been why they left Agnes to her own devices like that. It was one thing to want a head start in order to disappear, but quite another for them to lock her away in a cabin where she might never be found.

He had to keep his wits about him now and not lose his temper over them. They'd be found. He'd have the guards report back to the king and they could then take up the trail. For now, he would see to it that his beloved wife healed and could find a way to feel safe again.

The sun was just setting as they reached the inn. He thought of her alone in that cabin in that place where most of the locals would not go. He shook his head as he thought about the wildcat. Leave it to Agnes to befriend a wild animal to aid her. For surely she must be part faerie herself to have conjured such a thing. Now that was a story they would tell in time.

Having asked to have a bath sent up and word sent to Mugdock, they sat together in the largest chamber available and waited for the servants.

"Agnes, look at me," he said. She was pale and disheveled with her gaze cast downward. He understood all too well the depths one's mind could fall to when having suffered trauma like she had.

Slowly, she looked up until she met his gaze. The pain and sadness he could see behind her lovely eyes made his heart ache. He reached up to push some of her hair from her face.

"Agnes, I am here. You are safe."

Tears welled in her eyes and spilled onto her cheeks. "I know it, but I don't trust it," she whispered.

The servants arrived with a bath, steaming water, and a fresh shift and gown they placed on the bed. William helped her out of her soiled shift and promptly threw it on top of the fire. It disintegrated almost immediately.

He washed her limbs gently and then her hair and back. He hummed quietly to her to hopefully help her nerves settle as he softly wiped the blood from her fingernails where she'd tried to claw at the door. When she was fully washed, he had her lean back so he could brush her tangled hair. Her eyes were heavy as he sat with her, not wanting to disturb her or push her to talk if she did not wish it.

If she needed to focus inwardly, he would not push her otherwise. She was here and she was alive, and for now that was all he cared about. The rest would come in time, and they had plenty of it.

When the water cooled, he lifted her out of the tub and dried every inch of her and pulled the clean shift over her body. He sat with her in his lap by the fire until her hair was completely dry then brought her to the bed and tucked her in. William stripped then crawled in behind her and curled into her.

They stayed together like that for a long time. He knew her well enough to know she wasn't asleep and though he still wanted to ask her so many questions, some important as they might give clue to where Elspeth and John had gone, he would wait until she was ready.

Eventually, she turned to him and placed her hand on his cheek. Her tears flowed freely. He held her as her body released weeks of pent-up tension. She sobbed, which made him ache to take away the terror she must have felt wondering if she'd ever be found.

"William," she whispered. "You are really here?"

"Aye, my love. I am really here, and you're safe."

"William, I have something to tell you," she said.

His heart squeezed tight as he braced for bad news. He feared he would not be able to stand hearing of any abuse she might have endured, but he would remain strong for her sake. She needed that from him now.

"Go ahead, love. You can tell me anything and it will not change my love for you."

A faint smile crossed her lips. "I am with child," she said in a soft voice.

That voice, those words were like they'd been spoken by an angel.

"You are certain?" he asked trying not to explode with joy.

"Aye, I am. Are you pleased?"

"I have never heard of anything that gave me more joy other than the day you agreed to be mine."

She kissed him on the cheek and snuggled into him. Before long, her breath evened out and she snored lightly. William didn't sleep for many hours after that, pondering the future joy they would share together and how distinctly the stakes for their safety had changed.

CHAPTER TWENTY-TWO

AGNES WOKE WITH a start and bolted upright. The walls around her looked different, but she was convinced she was still in that God-awful cabin until strong arms wrapped around her and a familiar scent of leather and the outdoors enveloped her. William.

She leaned into him and let him pull her down with him. He wrapped them up with the quilt and kissed the top of her head.

"Shh, love. I'm here and you're safe."

He could tell her that all day long, but it would not quell the fear threatening to overcome her every time she closed her eyes that she would wake in that place. Despite having enough food and water and all her attempts to remain hopeful, the truth of the matter was when William called her name, she was certain it was her mind having completely snapped. Five days may not seem like a long time, but when one had no idea if they would ever be discovered, it might just as well be five years.

She hated this.

Agnes snuggled into William even harder as if his presence alone could remove the anguish welling inside. No amount of sobbing could easily erase despair once its claws set into one's heart like fingers of mist creeping down over the mountains, edging ever closer until all-consuming.

She closed her eyes and focused on William again. In her

mind's eye, she forced memories of their first meeting, their first kiss atop their horses, their wedding night. Wrapping her arms around him, she drank in his scent, willing it to bring her back to herself. By God, she would not let this claim her. She had to find a way out of this darkness.

As if sensing what she needed, William leaned down and brushed his lips across hers. She returned the kiss with all the urgency and yearning she'd felt while they were apart. Waking up alone in that horrible place broke her heart a thousand times over. But she was there no longer. She struggled to put herself in the here and now with this man and their bairn growing inside her.

Agnes pushed him to lie on his back and straddled him. She splayed her hands across his chest while he lifted her shift up and as she lifted her arms, he pulled it over her head. His hands reached for her breasts and squeezed. Her body reacted immediately.

Lifting her hips, she positioned herself so he slid in completely. Agnes tossed her head back as the sensation poured through her veins like liquid fire. William grabbed her hips to temper her movements when she started to ride him too hard.

"Slowly, love," he said as he guided her body to a delicious rhythm.

This, what they shared, was the only medicine that would cure her. This connection would block out any other feelings. It had to, for there was nothing she'd ever felt in her life more powerful than this.

Higher and higher she climbed trying to go faster, but William held her tight whispering soothing words, as if he understood this act and the love they shared could purge anything vile from her mind.

When she was sure she could take no more, and her mind was consumed only with him, he withdrew and flipped her onto her back and lifted her legs to wrap around his waist. William kissed her with such a passion as he entered her again with a hard thrust, withdrew, and slammed hard into her again. He did this so many times, she did not know how she'd survive her climax.

When it came, she tossed her head back and squeezed her eyes tight.

"Look at me," he said.

She opened her eyes as his climax overtook him. Her body and his quaking together, Agnes felt hope for the first time since leaving the great hall at Mugdock Castle all that time ago.

William did not pull out of her right away when they were finished. He lay on top of her and held her face in his hands. He kissed her forehead, her cheeks, her nose, and then her lips.

"Do you know how much you mean to me?" he said, gazing intently into her eyes.

She felt cherished in that moment.

"I believe it might be as much as you mean to me," she whispered.

"We have this, you know," he said as he pulled her to lie on her side facing him and stroking her hair.

"I do."

"And no one can ever take it away."

She started to understand a little of where he steered the conversation.

"You and I can be separated by all the demons in hell, and we would still have this. Do you understand, Agnes?"

She thought she did, but it was hard to pull oneself out of complete and utter despair. Had they taken a step in the right direction? Aye. But that didn't extinguish it like blowing out a candle.

"William, I cannot explain what it was like."

"I know, love. And you don't have to talk about it now. Only when you're ready. But you do understand it will help."

"Aye, I do know that. I suppose I'm trying to sort it all out for myself, before I can talk about it. What it was like waking each day, still in captivity, was bad enough, but then being in that place alone unable to leave. It was a nightmare from which I could not wake."

William held her tighter. "What can I do?"

"There's little you can do, besides give me time to work this through. And maybe—"

Agnes reached her hand down to feel him again. He was already coming to life once more.

"Och, but you are insatiable," he said as he rolled her to her back and quickly entered her.

This time was hard and fast, which was exactly what she needed to further purge those awful memories away. She understood they had a gift, and at the moment she was grateful for it for so many reasons.

Falling onto his back William turned his head to her. "Are you telling me, I am your medicine? Because och, love. I'll happily comply."

Agnes smiled at his enthusiasm. She supposed there could be worse medicines than an amorous husband who would move heaven and earth for her.

"Aye, now can we please leave this place? The last thing I need is to see wooden walls."

William didn't seem to need any further encouragement. He hopped out of bed and quickly gathered up their belongings, finishing with the strings on her gown the owner had provided for her. Within the hour they were atop his horse once more and riding hard for Mugdock Castle.

The wind in her face and the thick muscled chest at her back further aided in her spirits. When the castle walls finally came into view, she was certain she'd never seen a more joyous vision in her life. Once inside the gate, William's mother and brothers came running up to see her together with a sheepish-looking Neville.

"My dear, we were so worried. You have to know I prayed for you every night and my dearest assured me you would be saved. Well, here you are and you are looking quite gaunt. Now come and let us get you fed and rested."

His mother practically barked orders for anything she could think of apparently to see to Agnes's comfort. Agnes had never seen her so focused on anything besides her departed husband. Perhaps this whole business might help in her healing as well.

"Did the stories help?" she asked William after she finished issuing orders.

"Aye, mother. Right down to the very last one."

"You cannot mean…"

"Aye. They had a rustic cabin at the Devil's Pulpit."

Agnes's belly lurched at the thought, and she spewed her guts on the ground in front of her.

"Eww!" Geoffrey and Glenn said in unison.

"There now, do not fret. Let's get you inside. No more talk of your ordeal, my dear. And you two," she said to the boys. "See to it that's cleaned up."

They huffed and stomped their feet but headed toward the stable anyway. Agnes let William and his mother lead her to the great hall.

"Is it too much for you to be in here, love?" William asked when she stopped just inside the hall.

"I am well," she said. "But you might want to do something about those passageways."

"They're already sealed."

Good. That was one step closer to healing.

WILLIAM SEARCHED HIGH and low until he found the whittled figurines she'd tucked into her clothes chest. Gripping them tight, he brought them with him to their evening meal. She was home now, and he would do everything in his power to return them to where they were. With Elspeth, Connor, and John still at large and a significant complement of the king's guard still about, he vowed to distract her as much as possible.

They had not told his mother yet of her condition as truth be told, he rather enjoyed knowing that it was their secret alone. He didn't feel the threat was the same for them now as it had been, but it was not completely removed. The king had sent a missive stating how pleased he was Agnes had been found and that the majority of the rebels had given up once a few of them broke and revealed other names and locations. The whole thing had fallen apart pretty quickly after that.

So, was he still concerned? Aye. But the likelihood of anything further happening was beyond slim.

When he entered the hall, he found her sitting by the hearth with the boys on either side of her, all hunched over looking at something. He stopped for a moment to observe them. When he heard her laugh, his heart lifted. This would heal her. All of this; the love they shared, being around family. All of it. He was left in no doubt it would heal him too.

"She is a treasure, William. Surely there could be no other who would be better suited for you and for us."

He turned to see his mother standing beside him. She wrapped her arms around his middle which was something she hadn't done in many years.

"And how do you fare, Mother?"

"I am working through my mortification that my own daughter turned out to be such a monster and I didn't see it. All the signs were there for such a long time, and I was blind to it because of my own pain. I was unable to see any of yours, and for that I am so very sorry."

"You owe no one an apology, Mother, least of all me."

"Oh, but I do. William. You were left to pick up the pieces of this family when he died. I know you put your life on hold, and now you finally get to be happy." She shook her head and looked up at him with a watery smile. "I am so proud of the man you have become and the positive influence you will have on those boys and your own bairns."

Thoughts of the child growing in Agnes's belly made him

swell with pride. He hoped they would fill this castle with many in the years to come. He'd forgotten for the moment, his mother did not yet know.

"William, what is it?"

Just then Geoffrey came running up to them. "Mother, such a wonderful thing has happened!" Tugging on her arm, she looked at William with a furrowed brow and let her younger son pull her toward the hearth.

Agnes stood and faced her with her hand on her belly wearing a warm smile. William's heart was about to burst with the pride of her strength and his love for her.

With no words spoken, his mother understood immediately and raced over to embrace Agnes.

"Och, my sweet dear, is it true? And how do you feel? Are you wanting any particular food? Do you feel ill? Come and sit, and I will call for the cook. You must eat plenty of meat, for that is what will grow strong bairns. You are pale and so I will make sure we find pressed beetroot to drink." She drew in a breath and turned to William. "Go make sure Neville retrieves Old Nan. Tell her she has to move into the castle now. Tell her I said so."

William moved to Agnes and placed her figurines before her then smiled. "I'm sorry, there's nothing I can do for you now," he said with a grin. "She will give you no rest."

Agnes laughed and snatched up Bregdi and Nessie. "All is well," she said. "I don't mind a little pampering."

William kissed her soundly. "I will return soon. I have no idea what this evening's meal might include, but I suggest you select a sampling of all that is offered."

"If I do that, I'll be fat before I'm even showing," she said teasing him.

"There is no version of you I would not love and will not cherish."

With that he left the hall in search of Neville. He didn't have to look far as the man was just coming in through the gates. William didn't have to ask the gates be closed immediately anymore. It was a given until the order was lifted. If he ever allowed it again.

"Ah, there you are," Neville said as he dismounted. "I have news."

"As do I," William said with a grin. "Tell me yours first."

Neville cocked his head and raised a brow. "You're looking rather pleased with yourself today."

"Aye, now out with it so I can share mine."

"Very well, the buildings are nearing complete for the two families displaced. Several men from the town have offered to replace the furnishings if you can provide the materials."

"See to it they receive the best we can find as well as fabrics for bedding and clothing for all the family. I will pay for whatever they need."

"They will be pleased to hear it. So many in the town are grateful for your continued care and attention. You have well earned their respect over the years, but even more so now."

William wouldn't have it any other way. They were his people and he took his responsibility for them seriously."

"Now what is your news, or perhaps I can guess by the grin on your face."

"I won't make you guess, Neville. Agnes is expecting our first child."

William was pleased when Neville's eyes misted with his news. He'd mistakenly lost some faith in this man, but he intended to put it firmly back in place starting right now.

"Well, that is the best news I have heard in a long time. How is she?"

Chuckling, he said, "Suffering the very real peril of a doting grandmother to be. Which brings me to your assignment."

"Oh no. Something tells me I'm not going to like this."

"My mother's exact words were, '*Go make sure Neville retrieves Old Nan. Tell her she has to move into the castle now. Tell her I said so.*' And so you see, you get to bear the news, so I am saved," he said as he clapped Neville on the shoulder.

Neville's face paled. "You wouldn't do that to an old friend, would you?"

"I would not. Come, we ride together. She can refuse either of us individually, but she won't be able to resist both of us under my mother's orders."

Together they trotted to the village to speak with Old Nan trailing a cart for her comfort and belongings. William took the time to reflect on the time that had passed over the last several weeks. Like the town, his relationship with Neville would rebuild. As it would with his mother. He was pleased she had something else to focus on now, and perhaps in time she would spend more time with them than in the garden. The peace he'd always longed for appeared within reaching distance. They would need to stay the course, but he was certain with their collective effort they would come through this ordeal stronger than before.

That was all he could hope for at the moment. And that they all wanted the same peace gave him further hope. The king wanted his parties, and William wanted a quiet life. And why couldn't they both have that? His beloved Agnes would never feel fear for one more moment in her life or else he would slay the person who put it there. He'd found her by way of his own will and by the grace of God and he would never lose her again.

When they arrived at the village, William took his time to look around and truly see the extent of the damage. Those he encountered he spoke with at length to ensure they lacked nothing. He instructed the merchants to bring in extra provisions from wherever they could find them. His people would have fat stores from now on to help them heal as well. This horrible band of rebels had touched so many lives who would need justice, understanding, and support.

Now standing before Old Nan's home, he hesitated. He couldn't force the woman from her home. He didn't have the heart for that. So he would ask her kindly one more time and then if his mother wanted to take it up with her so be it.

When he was about to raise his hand to knock, the door

opened. She carried a bag and pointed to several crates behind her.

"Well, 'tis about time. I've been waiting all morning for ye. Come now, I will need to see to the lass to see what she's lacking. Come now, what's the hold up?"

Neville situated her in the cart, and they lifted in her life's collection of this and that. William scratched his head as she winked at him.

Would wonders never cease.

CHAPTER TWENTY-THREE

A S THE DAYS and weeks turned into months, Agnes's belly grew. She loved the feeling of her wee one kicking inside her. Well, except when they kicked her ribs. That part she did not care for so much. William's mother and Old Nan quarreled endlessly over what Agnes should eat or how often she should rest. Truly the most peace she achieved was on a daily stroll through the garden. There she talked to her little one and told stories of faeries and sea monsters and promised to share them all again once she was born. For Agnes was convinced she carried a wee lassie as sure as she drew breath.

William had cited no preference, for he looked at her each day she grew larger with a wide, wonderous expression. Not much could remove the smile from her face these days. Her time in the cabin felt like a bad dream she'd once had. Occasionally, she was surprised by an eerie feeling creeping over her, a little voice in the back of her mind telling her she would never be safe, and it was only a matter of time before she was abandoned again.

Thoughts of protecting her daughter kept those intrusions from doing any great harm. She was usually able to quell them and lock them into a box in her mind. Her nights were filled with pleasure in the arms of the most incredible man she'd ever been blessed to know. William was doting and loving and perfect. This life they'd carved between them would surely provide them with many wee ones who would thrive and fill this place with laughter and love.

Agnes sat on the bench William's mother usually occupied but could be found in less and less these days. She stared at the stone that had been somewhat worn from the many times a hand had rested there.

"She has been so good to me," Agnes found herself saying. "I hope my bairn will give her purpose. And I hope William and I will always love one another the way you both did. It was a sight to behold watching her come here to you all those times."

The wind picked up then, and some late-blooming rose petals loose from the bush separated and drifted to land at her feet. Agnes could not help but smile at the thought of William's father actually being connected to this exact spot. Perhaps his mother had been right all along. The thought warmed her heart.

Footsteps behind her drew her attention. She turned to find William wearing a solemn expression. Unease washed over her.

"Come, we should see you inside," he said as he approached.

"What is it? What's happened?" she asked.

"All is well. We are in no danger, but I have news you will wish to hear."

Agnes didn't know if she wanted to hear it or not. She accepted William's hand and followed him to the hall to where his mother and Neville waited.

"Where are the boys?" William asked.

"I have sent them to their chamber until we address this. They do not need to be a part of this vile business," his mother said.

"Mother, we should be grateful we have been asked our opinion. That was not required."

She stood and placed her hands flat on the table. Agnes had never seen the woman look so formidable. "You are correct, William. We should not have been asked. There is only one path forward and the king knows it. The decision should not be placed on us."

"Mother, I don't believe that is what this is about."

Agnes could take no more. "Will someone please tell me what this is all about?"

Neville stepped forward and pulled back a chair for her. He too had been quite doting on her and she'd grown to trust him as she had everyone else in the hall.

"I have heard from the king." William said.

"Aye, I gathered that much. And that it has to do with my uncle and your sister."

One did not need to be scholarly to glean what might upset them all so much.

"They have been captured. All three. They were found attempting to board a ship to Ireland in Prestwick."

"That is good news," Agnes said. The suspense was eating her alive. "So what has you all so riled?"

"They have been tried and found guilty of abduction and arson, both of which are treasonable offences and punishable by beheading."

Agnes was aware of that. Truth be told it had crossed her mind once or twice during her own captivity. "And?"

"The king is sensitive to the family relationship of all three and so asked our opinion of whether or not to carry out that sentence, or to instead imprison them at Edinburgh Castle."

Agnes sat back for a moment. From what his mother said, it would appear she was not pleased with the question either or its implications. She supposed having the decision to, or even voicing an opinion on such a matter, made oneself somewhat accountable. Never in her life had she considered someone else's life would be placed in her hands. Never mind how careless they'd been with her life.

She was not like them.

What right did she have to give someone life or take it away? Agnes placed her hand on her belly and rubbed up and down. She was put on this earth to create life. If she were to take it away from someone else, this beautiful miracle that grew within her would be somehow tainted.

But did they deserve life?

Even a cold rotten existence in Edinburgh dungeon was still life and the question remained: did they deserve even that? Considering the condition they'd left her in, a prison would be fitting. She'd been left to find pots and pans to relieve herself in for five days. No wonder William had covered his nose after he'd broken down the door. She had been overjoyed to be saved but horrified to have been found by him in such a state. If she ever had any doubt about his love and devotion, it was forever eliminated in that moment.

They wanted her to decide.

Agnes stood and pushed in her chair. She had been asked the most difficult question of her life and she would answer it. She had worked too hard to quell her fears over the past months and let only joy replace former anguish and darkness.

She would not let the dark in again.

"There is only one conclusion I can come to with such a request. The king, while making decisions like these as part of his role, must understand how difficult this is for us."

"I believe he surely does, Agnes," William said quietly as he placed his hand on her shoulder.

She placed her hand on his and smiled at him with all the love in her heart. She had no room left for evil. And she knew her place as a countess, a soon-to-be mother, and as a wife. At some point she would tell this story, together with William, to their children. She would have to look them in the face and be proud of the words she chose so carefully now.

Agnes was finally, after all this time, at peace.

"I do not believe any one person in this room possesses the authority to claim the life of another. The king has only been bestowed that right by the grace of God. You will write to his majesty and inform him that the duty to decide sentencing and the fate of Elspeth and Connor Munroe, and John Sinclair rests with him. We shall remain loyal servants to Their Majesties and respect this and future decisions he makes per his station as our sovereign."

She waited for debate. For one of them to disagree with her inherent belief that this decision had no place at this table and in either of their hands. It would forever connect them to this business and for her sake and the sake of all of them, she wanted to move on from this darkness.

William wrapped his arms around her and embraced her tight. "I have never been prouder of you or any other person in my life," he said.

And that right there was how she would tell the conclusion of their incredible tale.

SEALING THE MISSIVE, he passed it to Neville who nodded and slipped it inside his tunic.

"Is this truly over?" William asked him.

"I believe it is," Neville said. "You have married the strongest woman in all of Scotland. You know that, aye?"

"I do."

William might have eventually come to that conclusion but was impressed with the clarity of mind displayed by his wife. Even his mother had no other opinion once Agnes had spoken her piece. And she was right. They did not have the right to make that choice, nor should they be burdened with the decision.

His newfound respect for his wife also extended to his king who, apart from a small council of aides, made these decisions alone, and he would not wish that for all the power in the world. Perhaps the grand balls the king threw were a way to temper the enormity of running a kingdom and facing impossible decisions like this every day.

William left his solar in search of his wife. When he found her, he reached for her hand.

"Come with me."

He led her to the gates of the castle. "Open them," he ordered the guards.

When the deed was done, he turned to Agnes. "They shall remain that way from now on."

She looked at the gates and back to him, beaming. Drawing a deep breath, she said, "William, I am so very grateful for you. For what we will build here together."

William placed a hand on her round belly. He couldn't get enough of touching her, as if that act helped his own mind convince him all this was real. The bairn kicked, which William could only describe as a delightful sensation!

"He approves!"

"He?"

"You do not think 'tis a he?"

"I do not," she said and pinched his hand.

"What makes you think so?"

He didn't mind. He'd have a hundred wee lassies if they could.

"What do you think the king will decide?" she asked quietly.

"I confess, I do not know. I suspect he grappled with that himself which might be why he sought our counsel."

"I didn't think a king would ask such a question."

William shrugged. "He asks for input of his closest allies from time to time as a good king should. But the final decision rests with him."

He wasn't sure that made sense to her, for she appeared to see the topic more in black and white versus the various shades of gray making up the complexities of leadership.

"Either way, it is out of our hands now, and you and I have more pressing matters to attend."

"We do?"

"Aye, my beautiful wife. We have to decide which of the chambers will belong to this child," he said pointing his finger to her belly. "I suggest we make our way to the village and see what might spark your interest by way of inspiration."

He loved the way she squeezed his hand as she nodded. She was too far along to ride horseback so he had Neville ready the carriage and he would ride with her. And then another thought occurred to him.

"Wait right here," he said and left her standing by the carriage.

He found his mother and Old Nan in the great hall, bickering as usual over Agnes.

"Ah, there you two are," he said. "Come with me. We are taking Agnes to the village for the afternoon so she can choose fabric and give some instruction for the furniture for the bairn's chamber."

"She shouldn't be bounced around like that right now," Old Nan said shaking her head, though she still made her way toward the door. Was there a little spring in her step?

"She should be as active as possible which will help with the delivery," his mother said and walked fast enough to overtake the elder woman.

The two had forged a strong bond over these weeks through a common goal of a healthy and happy Agnes. Though William had to admit, the disagreements between them could be rather trying. Still, he'd take their current situation any day as it led to all their future joy and happiness. He could only imagine how they would be once the child was born.

They spent a lazy afternoon in the village. William was proud to give Agnes the full tour and introduced her to as many villagers as he could find. She'd met some before at the castle, but this was how he wanted them to mingle, in their element. And they were all so proud to show her what they could do.

By the time they were to return to the castle, Agnes had all the fabric arranged for the bedding, the design set for the bed and wardrobe, and tapestries ordered for the walls. Either his son would grow fond of soft colors, or Agnes was correct and the wee bairn would be a lass after all.

Though the distance to the castle was not far, the soft rocking of the carriage lulled her to sleep. William watched as she rested her head on his mother's shoulder. The latter beamed with pride and lifted her chin toward Old Nan who sat beside William.

"She had a good day," he whispered.

"Aye, the exercise was good for her. I recommend it twice a week."

"She will need to lie in very soon so I agree, but once a week will be enough."

He chuckled to himself. These two were impossible, and he was sure they would argue over the shade of blue in the sky.

At the castle, William lifted Agnes from the carriage and made his way to their chamber. He would let her rest and bring up a trencher for her later. Sitting by the fire and watching her sleep was the most peaceful thing in the world.

He thought back over their time together which had been filled with danger, passion, and adventure. Surely, they would have many stories to tell their own children and theirs again. He couldn't wait to tell of the brave lass who took on an entire rebel band, aiding in dismantling them. Of how she charmed him into falling so hard for her, he didn't know up from down. He'd tell of how she could bring magic into this world, simply by being the light others followed. He would follow her anywhere. He knew that now. From the moment he first laid eyes on her, he fell under her spell. They didn't need stories of fantastical beings to demonstrate the wonders of the world. She was it—all of it. She was the wonder in this world.

"You seem deep in thought," she said.

He looked up to see her watching him.

"Aye," he said as he crawled onto the bed beside her. "I was thinking what a fortunate woman you are to have a man such as me."

She rolled her eyes and swatted his arm. "I know you well enough to know you are not so vainglorious as to think that."

He chuckled and nuzzled her neck. "You know me too well. I

was thinking how fortunate I am to have found you. Truly, you make my life complete. This bairn," he said rubbing her belly, "will be the first of many. We shall have our own army of storytellers."

"And which stories shall we tell them?" she said turning toward him.

He loved the delight that rested on her face. "We shall tell them of a fearless lass who took on the devil himself."

Agnes winced and he immediately regretted making light of that ordeal. "Shh, love, I am sorry. It might be too soon to tell that tale." She nodded so he continued. "I shall tell of an enchantress who entered a king's hall in search of a heart to steal. And that the heart she found was gifted to her for all time."

"I like that story," she said. "Tell me more."

"Oh, this was no ordinary enchantress. She was forged from the sea and shaped by the north winds, an enchantress so powerful, no man could resist her."

"And then?"

"And then she met a devilishly handsome earl who swept her off her feet and they had twenty-four bairns and lived happily ever after."

Agnes swatted him again, but then soundly kissed him.

"Twenty-four, you say?"

"At least."

"Well then we must practice for when this one is born."

"Ye'll get no argument from me," he said as he pulled her to sit atop him.

Many hours later as she lay full and sated in his arms, he looked upward and thanked God for this, the most precious blessing of his life. For there could never be a greater gift than finding one's perfect life partner.

EPILOGUE

S HE WAS THE size of a whale. That was the only way she could think to describe herself these days. For the first time in the past several months, William's mother and Old Nan had agreed on something. That Agnes was due any day. And her anxiousness grew by the minute. The fear of not knowing was the worst. How much pain would she feel, if some unforeseen problem might cause danger to her or the wee one. Both women also agreed, Agnes was in top health, and each took credit for it.

Whether it was from her regular walks or the enormous amount of food they shoved at her, she had to admit, she felt well. But she'd been to a dark place in the past and she feared, as well she might return there after the bairn was born, as she was aware that could happen to some mothers.

Agnes had not shared any of her fears with anyone because they appeared worried enough. While she was in the best hands possible, she understood all too well that so much could and sometimes did go very wrong.

As she sat on the bench in the garden the sound of a chiffchaff echoed around her. Usually the first birds she heard in spring, the sound brought light to her heart. This wee creature reminded her that everything renews in spring. And she would too. As she stood to go find William, her waters broke, gushing down over her legs and feet. A stabbing pain ripped through her the moment it happened and she doubled over.

"Oh!"

The first pain passed and she was able to stand upright to find William running toward her.

"Agnes!"

"The babe comes," she said through clenched teeth. "Help me inside."

William made to lift her but she stopped him. "No, let me walk. It will help."

Another contraction overtook her and she doubled over again. When she looked up, his mother and Old Nan were making their way to her.

"You had better get her inside quickly," his mother said. "I wrote to her mother months ago and asked what her deliveries were like and her reply said they were swift and excruciating. We don't have much time so unless you want her to birth this child here on the lawns for all to see, you need to get her inside."

Agnes wasn't sure she liked the descriptors her mother used. There was no way to predict how a woman's labor would transpire. But this pain was intensifying and when William picked her up, she was sure she would faint in his arms.

But she held on. High above her the chiffchaff called to her, reminding her of her purpose and responsibility to the wee one about to come into the world. Agnes focused on the bird's call each time a new contraction swept over her. By the time they reached her chamber, she was bathed in sweat. His mother and he helped her out of her gown and into a birthing shift and then into bed. Once she was off her feet, she felt a little better and the contractions gave way to brief moments where she could catch her breath and prepare for the next.

William mopped her brow like she'd done for him all those months ago when he was racked with pain from a poisoned arrow. She remembered how helpless she felt and by the look of concern on his face now, he might be feeling that same helplessness keenly.

The next contraction brought with it an overwhelming need to push.

"Not yet, lass," Old Nan said as she checked to see how far Agnes had advanced. "You must let the next couple happen without pushing. Talk to her, laddie. Keep her mind occupied. If she pushes too soon, the babe will tear her apart."

The pain meddled with her ability to comprehend, so great with the pressure building beyond her ability to resist.

He sat beside her and held onto her as the pain made her body shake. "Do you remember Fin?"

She nodded through her breathing. His mother was on the other side of her demonstrating how to control inhaling and exhaling and Agnes focused hard on just that.

"Fin has sent us a gift for our wee one that we three will open together as soon as he's here. Come on, wee laddie," he said.

She knew he was jesting to try to distract her, but it was of no use. She tilted her head back as the next contraction hit. She couldn't survive much more of this and now understood why women fell into darkness from this process. How could one not feel violated by something that was supposed to be precious and magical?

Doubt crept into her heart. Wasn't she supposed to be over-joyed right now? There was no joy in her heart as the old woman kept her from doing what her body so desperately wanted. She began to resent them all then. How could they allow this torture to continue when relief was so close at hand?

"Surely she must be ready to push now. Can't you see how much agony she is in?"

Willam's words mirrored her own thoughts which had now turned as dark as they'd ever been. She'd already failed this child and William for not being able to withstand the pain that came with bringing her into the world. She was angry with God who had blessed her with such a gift but at the cost of her own self-worth.

A small bird flew in through the window and landed atop the

wardrobe as if to further mock her.

Agnes sat up a little. "I will be pushing on this next wave, so you had better be ready," she said with far more assertion than any words she'd ever spoken before.

William held her tighter as the old woman nodded. "You are as ready as you could ever be. When I tell you, I want you to push down hard and stop when I tell you. Do you understand?"

"Aye." She would listen as long as they were moving forward.

When the next wave came, the old woman called out. "Push!"

Agnes leaned forward with her chin on her chest and pushed with all her might. "Stop!"

The woman placed her hand on Agnes's leg. "That was really good, lass. One more will do it. Are you ready?"

Agnes brought her head forward again and nodded. She had no strength for words. All of it would be used to bring her bairn into the world.

"Push!"

And push she did. With all the strength she could muster, she envisioned her child's head coming out. That alone released an enormous amount of pressure.

"Stop now. One more and your wee one will be here."

Agnes focused on the old woman as if no one else was in the chamber with them. The bird called from the wardrobe just as the final wave hit and she could hear the word "Push!"

As the bairn came into the world, Agnes was vaguely aware the bird flew back out through the window and all the pressure in her body released. The old woman lifted the child upside down and waited.

The lone cry washed over Agnes in a shower of light. All doubt washed out of her mind and her heart in a second. The old woman placed the wee one on Agnes's chest as she wiped the child down and made to cut the cord.

Once that was done Agnes looked down at her precious angel surely sent from God, despite her earlier doubt.

"Well," William said. "Is it a laddie or a lass?"

She didn't have to look, but she did. This ferocious lass would claim the world as her own; Agnes was as sure as she existed.

"She's a bright wee lassie to be sure," she said to him as he lifted the blanket from her face.

Sleepy eyes met Agnes's gaze as a little hand curled around her finger. She was lost in the power this little one held over her. The old woman and William's mother shooed him out as they set to clean her up and ensure she would heal properly.

Now seated in a chair by the hearth and wearing a clean nursing gown with the maids stripping the bed, Agnes would never tire of staring at this darling little one who had taken all the broken pieces inside her and mended them together with one small cry.

Much later, after they helped her nurse for the first time, she lay in bed with the bairn between her and William. A cradle rested by her side for the nighttime feedings. She had all sorts of offers to assist her with aspects from changing nappies to finding a nursing maid from the village.

Agnes didn't want any of that. All she wanted now was for this peace in her heart to remain for all time.

When she looked up from staring at her daughter, it was to find William staring at her. "I saw the moment you changed," he said.

"How do you mean?"

"You struggled and I could feel your pain rolling off you in waves. I wanted so desperately to take that pain from you, but you sank deeper into it. When she made her first cry, your whole body changed. It was as if a dark cloud had been lifted from you forever. Your body relaxed into mine for the first time in a long time."

"I admit, I was having some doubt."

"Aye, and I'm glad this was not Nan's first birthing," he said as he moved some of the babe's blanket from her face.

She was absolute perfection as she lay there sleeping soundly swaddled in a soft linen blanket.

"Do you have a name in mind?" she asked him, understanding the responsibility to his family with their first born.

"I shall ask you to do that honor, Agnes. I believe you have earned that right."

She didn't have to think long on it. For during all these months there was only one name that came back to her time and again.

"Her name is Morag."

His teeth glinted in the candlelight from his broad smile. "Well, that sure is fitting. The Star of the Sea? Aye, I couldn't imagine you coming up with any name better."

"And I could not imagine a more perfect family. Truly, William. We are so very blessed. And should you ever find that I carry darkness in my heart, please come and talk to me. You will get through to me; I know it now."

"That I promise you, with all my heart."

How long they lay there on that first night she would never be able to say. But as the sun rose and she'd nursed Morag twice more that night, she vowed she'd never forsake the blessings that had been bestowed upon them ever again.

They'd opened Fin's gift which was a dove with a small branch in its beak carved from stag antler. A beautiful sentiment of purity, love, and new beginnings.

With William snoring in their bed and Morag quietly snuggled into her arms, Agnes stared out through the window. The birds were just waking and more than one stopped by to land on the windowsill as if to pay homage to this new miracle they had witnessed. The world was a brighter place today with a new child to celebrate. Before long, their lives would become hectic with more bairns and more commotion in the castle.

Agnes would impress this moment upon her heart and soul for all time. This was her shield to ward off any darkness ever threatening to creep into her heart and mind in the future. She had not failed as a mother. It was to be her strength and with that came a renewed sense of herself. A love she had lost but that now returned with a vengeance. When she heard the chiffchaff's call this time, it was to celebrate her own renewal.

THE END

Acknowledgements

To my sons who watch me slip into an alternate human form to create the stories I adore so much—you are the reason I want to succeed. I love you both so much for your unwavering love and support.

To Kathryn and all the team at Dragonblade, thank you for welcoming me into the fold and responding to all my questions. I feel truly blessed to be a part of the family.

To Michelle O. Always, always, always for offering your keen eye and insightful advice to a stubborn writer. You help make me readable and link everything together when I don't know how. Thank you.

To Melanie and Vicki. Thank you for cheering from the bleachers as always!

To my beta readers, Vanessa, Sam, and Cynthia. Thank you for your feedback on the advanced read. I love your encouragement and thoughts about what's working and what's not. I could not have finished this story without your encouragement and accountability.

To my readers. Thank you for taking a chance on a little maid from the Cove all those years ago and for putting up with me delving into a new series before finishing the last one. I will get to it, I promise. You have reached out to me many times over the years with helpful critique and kind words and your support has been a source of inspiration. I sincerely hope you enjoy *A Courtship in the Highlands* and I will continue to work hard to provide you with good quality entertainment. Please keep reaching out over all my platforms.

Much love to you all!!!

About the Author

Amazon internationally bestselling author of the award-winning Highland Chiefs series, Kate Robbins writes historical romance out of pure escapism and a love for all things Scottish. She thoroughly enjoys the research process and delving into secondary sources in order to blend authentic historical fact into her stories. Ranging over a thousand years, Kate's novels are filled with passion, adventure, and political intrigue. Kate is the pen name of Debbie Robbins who lives in St. John's, Newfoundland and Labrador, Canada.

Facebook:
facebook.com/KateRobbinsA

X:
x.com/KateRobWriter

Instagram:
instagram.com/robbins.kate

BookBub:
bookbub.com/authors/kate-robbins

Amazon:
amazon.com/Kate-Robbins/e/B00FRHRUPE

YouTube:
youtube.com/channel/UCpmDa4KgxFVKqoTK0CS6SRg

Goodreads:
goodreads.com/author/show/7328484.Kate_Robbins

TikTok:
tiktok.com/@robbins.kate